THE DEVOURED AND THE DEAD

KRISTOPHER RUFTY

DEATH'S HEAD PRESS
an imprint of Dead Sky Publishing, LLC
Miami Beach, Florida
www.deadskypublishing.com

ISBN: 9781639510085

First Edition

Cover Art: Justin T. Coons

The "Splatter Western" logo designed
by K. Trap Jones

Book Layout: Lori Michelle
www.TheAuthorsAlley.com

SPLATTER
WESTERN

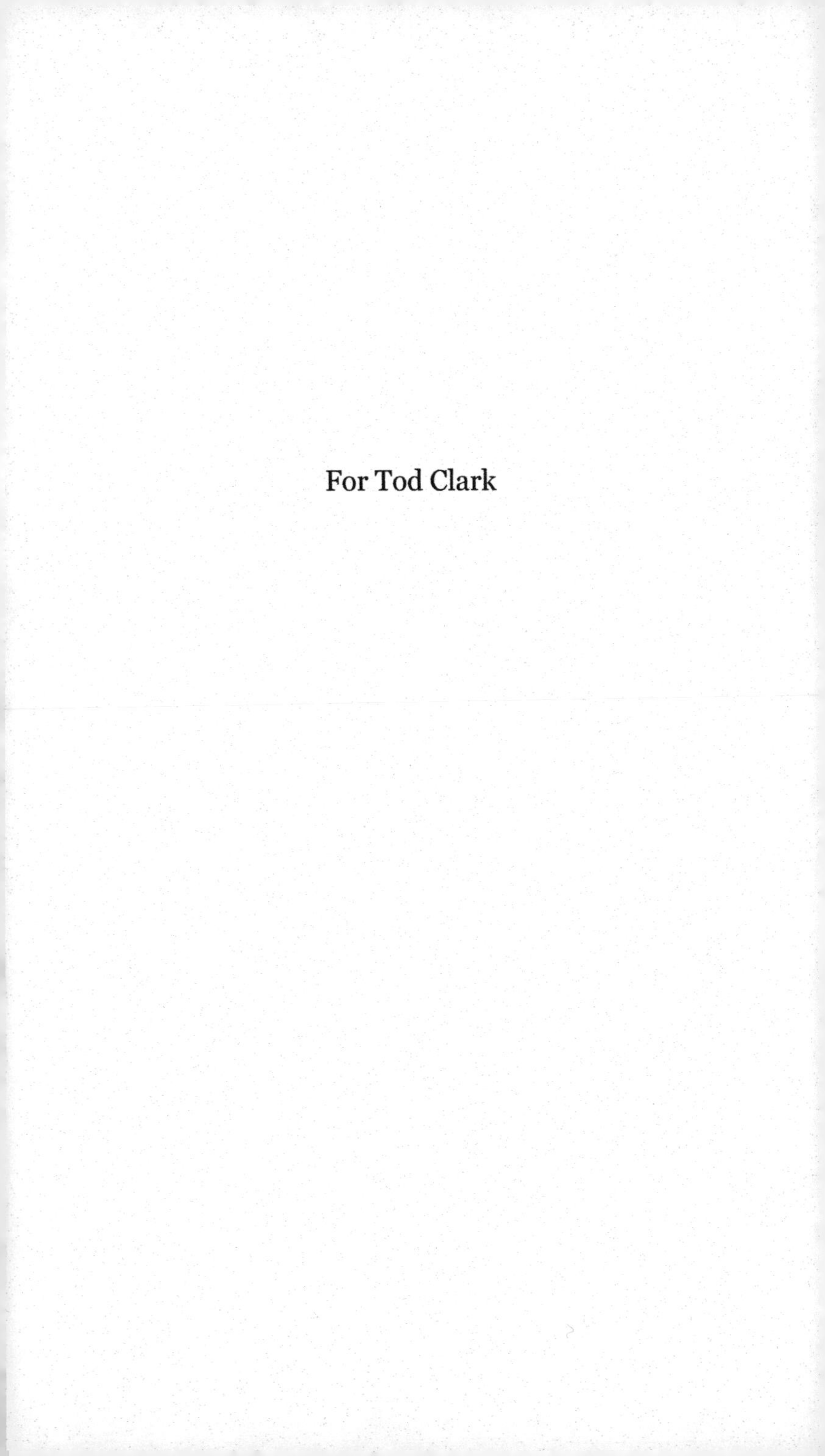

For Tod Clark

1

THEY ATE THE BABY.

Even all these years later, I am still haunted by the crunchy smacking sounds their mouths made as they gobbled the cooked flesh. And how the huffs that sputtered through their noses turned to fog in the cold air.

I probably shouldn't begin the narrative there. What an awful way to start. That's where my mind always goes first whenever I allow it to remember what happened. Sure, there is more story to tell leading up that moment, but it hardly seems important to the story that follows.

That's where it really began for me.

Maybe some brief backstory would suffice? I've only recounted the story a few times before, all details intact. But those early sections are greying. Soon, they will be black. My mind does that now, it seems. Shuts down for periods of time, and when it comes back there are these blank spaces where a memory used to be.

But the smell of the baby's meat roasting over the fire, blending with the frozen scent of the ice and snow-drenched forest around us, remains a vivid nightmare that I cannot seem to lose in those dark spaces my mind creates.

I remember the snow. I remember the blood. I remember the death.

I remember the feeding.

Perhaps that's not where this recollection should begin for you. I'm not an author. I have read books and have enjoyed them while trying to learn the craft. Maybe there is no craft. Maybe there is only the story and how it's told.

How should I tell this one?

Maybe you want to know who all was there before the story unfolds. That would most likely be crucial to your understanding the details of the rest. A story should introduce you to the people in it. This story should be no different. How else will you appreciate the calamity of those affected if you don't first know who they are?

My name is William "Billy" Coburn, and it was the dead of winter in 1884. I was eleven years old when we were stranded deep in the dead heart of Mountain Rock, a scarcely populated and traveled precipitous area. There were four families: mine, the Coburns, which consisted of Mama (Claire) and Daddy (Abe), myself, and my sister, Lenora. She was sixteen and helped Mama run the house. At times, it felt as if I had two mothers always nagging me.

Two of the other families were the Shumakers and McCrays, and just like us, they'd sold off their farms to relocate to a place called Harvest Hill. It had been an antiquated mountain town until somebody struck gold. Daddy had learned about it in the paper. Lots of folks were planning to go out there that spring and stake their claim.

And our families wanted their fair share.

The Shumakers were the largest of the families,

with three kids—the twins Jonathan and Janey were the same age as my sister. We all just sort of expected Jonathan and Lenora would marry at some point. Our families had been grooming them for it since birth, and Jonathan seemed just fine with a predestined life with my sister. Lenora, though she liked Jonathan, didn't seem keen on settling down with anybody.

Lenora was more than a sister to me. Looking back on it, I see she had branded herself my guardian. Something different than Mama and Daddy. Someone I was even closer to than them. She knew I would need her, but I don't think even she realized just how much I would need her over those long days when we were trying to stay alive.

I'm doing it again, aren't I? Jumping around. I get that way. I know I promised to tell it, and I will. But I need to tell it the accurate way. If I go too fast, I will leave out too much. But if I don't hurry up and get to it, I will find myself unable to carry on.

Where was I?

I started to tell you about the Shumakers. I guess that's a good place to continue. The twin sister, Janey, kept to the house, mostly doing chores and assisting Mrs. Shumaker with all her duties. Everything that boys liked about my sister was lost on poor Janey. She wasn't ugly by any means, but where Lenora seemed to cast a brightness that outshined sunlight whenever she smiled, Janey's face was plain and dull, with large teeth that caused her lips to bulge. Her body was flat all around, long arms and legs that had little meat on them. But Lenora was lean, tough, and beautiful. More than once I found myself ready to pound on a boy for the way he looked at my sister.

I doubted Janey's brothers ever had to worry about that.

Though she and Jonathan were twins, they looked nothing alike. Seemed as if all the good genes were mugged by Jonathan in their mama's womb. He came out an unflawed creation. And Janey came out a tedious imitation, devoid of even a nuance of personality. To be honest, I wouldn't have been surprised if she honked like an ass instead of speaking a human language.

As bad as Janey was, she was nowhere near as awful as James. He was fourteen and plump. His flat hair draped his forehead above his eyebrows. There were times when his mass would rip right through the fabric in pasty bulges. I despised everything about him from his disgusting eating preferences to his annoying voice that always seemed to be a whiny squeal no matter the mood he was in.

And yet, he was the only friend I had.

But we weren't *really* friends. Our age difference made it hard to have much in common. However, we settled for existing without trying to kill each other. It was just easier that way.

Then there were the McCrays, the most hated family in town. They were also the wealthiest and didn't mind telling you about it whenever they got the chance. Even when they didn't have the chance, they still managed to brag about it in some manner. It was a natural gift that Jack and Mary McCray possessed.

At the time, I wasn't able to come up with one logical reason for their wanting to scratch off the life they'd built and go elsewhere. Maybe they realized, rich or not, living in a town and being hated by everyone was just too dangerous. It could have been their way of fleeing without it looking as if they were running away.

As much as I despised them, I couldn't ignore their greatest quality: Ellie. She was their daughter. Two years older than me, she was everything her parents were not. Lovely to look at, with hair the color of a brushfire. She had a spill of freckles that covered her cheeks and connected at the bridge of her nose. How she was the offspring of a couple of cruel pricks like the McCrays never made any sense to me.

We knew each other a little, and I was eager to spend several weeks traveling with her, even if we were going to be doing so in the heart of the winter on separate carriages.

The travel arrangements were Jack McCray's idea. If we wanted to get there before the rush piled in, we needed to travel when nobody else would be. That would be our advantage, he'd said.

And everyone agreed, including Daddy.

I didn't know much about traveling conditions and how the weather affected it. I did know that going such a long distance and not knowing what we would have to face was not a smart decision. I didn't say that, though. I never went against anything Daddy decided. It wasn't as if he would beat me for having an opinion. I just figured if Daddy was all for it, then everything would somehow be just fine.

It was Daddy's idea to hire us an Indian guide—Ahote. Tall and muscular, he could have been carved from obsidian stone. Everything about his appearance seemed to declare strength and agility. He wanted to relocate as well with his wife and baby. He was happy to accept the job, so long as his family could come, and they could live in Harvest Hill with all of us. Plus, he'd done a lot of work for Daddy on the farm and we'd gotten to know them pretty well.

Chenona was Ahote's bride. They looked more like brother and sister than husband and wife. When I saw Chenona for the first time, my mouth went dry. My heart began to pound into my throat. I had never known such beauty in a woman could be real. Her skin was somehow dark and creamy all at once. Her hair, the color of a starless night, was shiny and sleek and hung far down her back. I noticed how all the men, including Daddy, looked at her when they didn't know anyone was watching them. As an old man now, I understand what must have been going through their minds.

So there's the four families, all joined together with one obstacle ahead of us. I wasn't too worried about things, but I also wasn't very excited about it.

2

DETAIL IS SOMETHING that I tend to dwell in. I've been accused of dragging out a story longer than it is needed to be. However, for this telling, I am not sure how much I should share. I could fill pages about the unnatural cold and heavy, never-ending snow alone. Years later, the winter we set out on our journey would be recorded as historical. So far, in my lifetime, only one winter has topped it in almost sixty years.

There was no way we could have known the bleak winter that awaited us.

There are so many areas I could elaborate in. I could do a complete account of every day we were out there. It's not necessary for this. I believe guiding this tale right to where it really began would be the best choice. There's no point in lingering or taking my time. All I would be doing is delaying matters, so I can avoid returning there in my mind. But, you see, I'm always there, even when I'm asleep. The screams, the blood, the tearing chomps of teeth and meat.

The copper odor of cold blood.

It haunts me.

God, help me through this.

Mr. McCray suggested we take the Broken Moon

Path. That route, though not ideal, would shave off several days of travel time. The plan was to ride into Harvest Hill as quickly as possible and hopefully ahead of any winter storms.

But we were hit by snow two days into the travel. It wasn't a bad fall, but it made the path harder to handle for our horses. There were three carriages. Ahote and Chenona had put their scant belongings on ours. Chenona rode under the cloth with Mama, Lenora, and myself. Mama even helped with the baby at times so Chenona could rest.

Ahote rode up front with Daddy, assisting him with navigating the horses. Since Ahote knew the way through Broken Moon Path, our wagon was the leader.

After a full day of travel, we finally got ahead of the snow. Things went fine for a while, but when we entered the mountains, another storm struck. The towering trees protected us from a lot of the downfall, but we still had trouble making any real progress. Our breaks were longer this time because the trek seemed to be hard on the horses.

That was when Chenona began all her talk about how we shouldn't have gone this route. Apparently, we should have followed where the trail branched to the left. Ahote had guided us straight.

"The snow," he'd said, "will not be as harsh here."

"What is she talking about?" Daddy asked. "Are we in danger?"

"No."

Chenona began to speak, but Ahote looked over his shoulder. His hard gaze silenced her. Then he faced forward again. I couldn't hear what he was saying to Daddy but could make out fragments over the squeaky roll of the wheels and the howling wind to put it all together.

He assured it might not be an easy trek, but it would be the safest one.

Chenona shook her head. She began to speak softly in her native tongue. Even in her panic, I thought it was beautiful, like everything else about her. She caught me watching her and heat spread through my cheeks.

She forced herself to smile. “It will be okay, handsome.”

That made my cheeks feel as if a match had been set to my skin. I nodded, then looked at Lenora, who was trying not to laugh at me.

Then Lenora suddenly shot off her bench and landed at my feet when the wagon rolled over a deep rut.

It was my turn to laugh.

Mama snapped her fingers at me. “Enough. Help me with your sister.”

I grabbed Lenora’s arm and pulled while Mama reached under her and lifted. Lenora dropped onto the bench with a grunt. “That smarts,” she said.

The ride went on like that. Sometimes, I would be knocked out of my seat. Once, Mama landed on her side at my feet. But none of us got hurt other than minor bruises and some cuts here and there. It seemed like Ahote was right, since nothing really harmful happened.

Then a couple days later, the first horse dropped dead. It was one of the Shumakers’ three that pulled their wagon. Nothing had seemed to be wrong with the mount before it happened. It just dropped and didn't get up.

Mr. McCray chalked it up to exhaustion and nobody disputed the idea since it seemed the most likely reason. We moved on, leaving the dead horse behind.

I thought that would be the worst of it.

Over the course of several days, we lost all the horses. First it was the Shumakers, who had to abandon most of their belongings with their wagon. We all took in what we could, including the Shumakers themselves. They hitched with the McCrays, except for Jonathan, of course. He rode with us, sitting awfully close to Lenora while sharing a blanket.

It happened with the McCrays right after. Their first horse dropped without any warning. None of us knew what to do as we stood around the dead animal. It looked as if it had simply fallen asleep while walking and collapsed.

We were deep in the wilderness at this point, surrounded by immense trees, devoid of all their leaves. The branches above us seemed to intertwine, tangling to form larger monstrous limbs.

I was staring up at those gnarly branches when Chenona tried to warn us again. This time, nobody was so quick to dismiss what she had to say.

"This land has seen much death," she said. "Our people said it's forsaken. Too many of our kind was slaughtered here. We keep going, it will be our deaths as well. They are warning us to leave this cursed place."

"Who is?" Mama asked.

"The evil ones."

McCray spat. The tobacco juice made a brown line on the snow. "Evil ones, bullshit! We've gone too far to head back, woman. It'd be our deaths for sure."

Ahote stepped in front of his wife. "We will continue forward. We are couple weeks' ride away from the pass. The travel will be much simpler and shorter from there."

McCray stared at Ahote. "You sure about that?"

Ahote nodded.

Daddy patted the tall man's shoulder. "I trust you, Ahote. You'll do right by what you said."

"It is my word," said Ahote.

Chenona's chin trembled. She turned away, carrying their baby back to the wagon.

But by the end of the next day, we had abandoned everything but what food supplies, guns, blankets, and garments we could carry. The McCrays and Shumakers were all stuffed inside our wagon. Our poor horses moved slower than time, but they did move.

At least, for a while.

We'd been traveling for eleven days when we set up camp for the night. We had three horses left. The snow had hardened to a crust. But the night was warmer than others had been, so we only kept a moderate fire going through the night. Daddy figured the snow would melt off in a couple days, and we would set back out when it was safer.

The sleeping arrangements were simple. The kids and women slept in the wagon with Chenona and the baby. Ahote stayed outside with the other men, sleeping alone by the fire while Daddy, McCray, and

Floyd Shumaker slept in crudely constructed tents they made of old blankets and sticks. Low to the ground, they were like small, crooked dens a fox might shelter in. A tattered curtain hung over the entrance, flapping in the wind. Whenever somebody needed inside, they had to crawl to enter.

Before I drifted off to sleep, I heard Ahote telling Daddy that if things wemt as well as they did today, we'd be in Harvest Hill in thirteen days. Then darkness spilled across me, smothering out my thoughts. I dropped into a hard, fitful sleep.

3

I AWOKE TO the sound of arguing. Sitting up, I shoved the blankets aside. Lenora was on all fours at the front of the wagon, pulling back the hammercloth to peer out. Jonathan, crouched beside her, looked over at me. He put a finger to his mouth to shush me.

I turned around and saw Janey next to James, her legs pulled to her chest and hugging them. The thick dress had pulled up to show bars of pale skin above her boots. James was still asleep, his large stomach rising and falling.

Chenona was in the back corner, sitting with her back to the wood. The baby, wrapped in a thick blanket, was pressed to the smooth mound of her breast. She wasn't looking at me. Her eyes were pointed down as she quietly tried to get the infant to suck.

I gulped. I forced myself to look away.

I spotted Ellie on her knees beside Lenora. Her cherry hair was mussed, hanging around her face in wild tangles. "What are they fighting about?" Ellie whispered.

"The horses are gone," said Lenora.

My growling stomach seemed to shrink. "Gone?" I said.

Jonathan tapped his mouth with his finger. I nodded. We all listened to McCray chastise Ahote. Apparently, it had been his turn to keep watch but he had fallen asleep. I could hear Daddy trying to be the voice of reason by pointing out it could have happened to any of us.

None of Daddy's reassuring efforts seemed to work, so he tried another method.

"All right, Jack," said Daddy. "That's enough. I've about had it with that mouth of yours. You open it again, I'm going to shove my fist down your gullet and pull your stomach out between your teeth."

"Abe!" Mama said.

Ellie looked back at me. At first, I thought she might be angry because of what Daddy said. Instead, it looked as if a smile was tugging the corners of her mouth. She'd probably wanted to say something similar to her old man many times.

McCray grumbled a bit outside, but I couldn't understand him. I could hear the crunches of his footsteps as he walked away.

"Where are you going?" Floyd asked.

"To find our damn horses," said McCray. "Their tracks go off this way."

"Hang on," said Daddy. "I'll go with you."

"Well, bless me," said McCray. "Praise the Lord that you're comin' along."

"Watch your tongue," said Daddy.

McCray harrumphed.

Lenora shook her head. "Too busy arguing to do anything."

Jonathan let out a deep breath. Eyes closed, he leaned back his head. Lenora turned around. Her nose was bright pink from being exposed to the cold air. It made the rest of her face look very pale. Her blue eyes looked to be the color of the ice outside.

"What's going to happen to us?" she asked. She didn't seem to be asking anyone particular. It was as if she'd accidentally spoken what she'd been thinking.

Jonathan shrugged. "I haven't a clue."

"Do you think somebody stole the horses?" Janey asked.

Jonathan shook his head. "Who would be out here in the middle of the night to do it?"

"Us," I said.

He frowned. "Other than us."

"Indians?" asked Ellie.

I glanced back at Chenona, hoping she hadn't heard Ellie's comment. The dark-skinned woman was shaking her large breast at the baby, making it jiggle. I glimpsed the dark coin of her nipple and felt a pull low in my abdomen. I looked back at the others.

"Doubtful," said Jonathan, answering Ellie's question. "They're mostly gone from here. They live together in different regions."

"But there are still some," said Ellie. "Daddy told me about savages and how they hide out in the trees like animals, waiting on white people to come along to kill. They don't kill the women or girls. They take them and . . . "

"Enough," said Lenora. "Little girls shouldn't talk about such things. And your daddy shouldn't be filling your head with that shit."

"I am *not* little," said Ellie, making her sound less mature than she actually was.

"I'm scared," said Janey.

“We all are,” said Lenora.

“Are we going to be trapped out here? We’ll starve . . . ”

“No,” said Jonathan. “I’m sure there will be some plan put into place. We have food.”

“Barely any,” I said. “I helped load it with you. There’s barely anything.”

Ellie let out a soft moan.

Lenora put her arm around the redhead’s shoulders. “Quiet, Billy. You’re scaring her.”

“I was already scared,” said Ellie. “Billy didn’t do it.”

Heat flowed up my neck.

Janey shoved her face into her hands and rubbed up and down. When she pulled them away, her face was ruddy. “I don’t want to be here. Stranded out here like a pack of outlaws hiding from the law.”

Jonathan sighed. His hair draped his forehead, the tips dangling in his eyes. I hoped I would be as handsome as he was when I got older. “We’ll be all right. It will be hard, but we will be fine.”

“Promise?”

Jonathan nodded. He looked at all of us. “I swear. We just have to trust that our parents will come up with some kind of plan. I’m sure they will.”

Nobody else said anything.

James began to stir, the blankets rustling as he stretched. He sat up. His oily hair stuck up in sections all over his head. He looked around at us. “What’s for breakfast?”

Before anyone could enlighten him to what was going on, Chenona bolted from the corner. She rushed to the front, crouching over, the baby close to her. She’d put away her breast.

"Ahote!"

She flung the curtain aside. Cold air rushed in.

"What's the matter?" Ahote said. His large shape appeared in the gap of grey light between the curtain, blotting out a large section of it.

"The baby! Something's wrong!"

4

I DIDN'T GET to see the baby until a little while later. We were all outside, eating a very small breakfast of ham and potatoes around the fire. We sat on logs we'd chopped from the woods.

The baby seemed okay, though there were purple blots in the corners of his eyes. He wouldn't open them, but seemed to react whenever Chenona spoke to him with slight head movements.

Seeing how much Chenona was crying made me want to cry to. My throat felt tight. It was hard to swallow. Mama held the Indian woman, her head pressed to Mama's chest as if she were a child as well. She hadn't even touched her food. I noticed James's eyes kept wandering to the uneaten meal on the plate.

Patty Shumaker held the baby bundled in blankets. She looked nothing at all like any of her children. Though I didn't know for sure, I assumed she was at least ten years younger than Floyd and could have passed for the older sister instead of the mother. "He's cold." She raised the baby to her mouth, kissed his forehead. She looked up, her lip clamped under her teeth. "His skin feels so cold."

Ahote was crouched by the wagon. Daddy stood

over him. He put a hand on the burly guide's shoulder.

Floyd Shumaker stood off to the side with the twins and James, while the McCrays kept their distance as well. Jack McCray puffed on a cigar, watching, his dark eyes narrowed. He had a mustache that formed a horseshoe around his mouth. Not much hair on top, but he made up for it with the bushy strip on the sides.

No one spoke. No one knew what to do.

"We leave now," said Ahote, standing up. He turned to Daddy. "I cannot wait any longer. My baby is sick."

"We will," said Daddy. "We have to get things in order first."

"Leave?" I said.

I looked at Lenora, sitting across from me. Her face had a puzzled expression as if this were her first time seeing any of these people.

Daddy nodded. "Ahote and I are going ahead on foot. We're bound to come across somebody the closer we get to the pass."

"Why don't all of us go, then?" asked Lenora.

"Ha," said McCray as if spitting the word. "You kids trying to make it through these woods? And toting around a sick baby, at that? The women? Hell no."

"We'd be all right," I said.

McCray leered at me. His head was covered in a wool cap that bulged on the sides. I was taller than him by a hair but still felt a tremor of fear inside by his gaze. "Oh? And my little girl? She'd be fine. And that fat boy?"

James gasped.

"Hey," said Floyd. "Don't you talk about my son like that." He stood up, placing his hands on his hips. He looked like a schoolteacher more than a farmer.

"Shove it in your ass, Shumaker. I'm just pointing out that it wouldn't be ideal to take these kids out into the cold, on *foot*. Your boy wouldn't make it a mile."

Mary McCray stood up from the log she'd been sitting on by the fire. It was easy to forget that she was there most of the time since she rarely spoke. But when she did, everyone listened. She was a short woman, almost frail, but her voice held a deepness to it that caught your attention. "That is enough, Jack. I've had it with the way you're talking to everyone. Close your mouth and leave it that way."

McCray spun around, his cheeks reddening. "You can't speak—"

Jonathan appeared behind Mary's shoulder, staring at Jack. "Shut up," he said. Jonathan had been sent out to look for the horses. I wasn't sure how long he'd been gone before returning.

McCray's mouth hung open. He turned to Floyd. "You going to let your boy talk to me this way?"

Floyd cleared his throat. "Jonathan. Sit down."

"Don't," said Daddy. "Jonathan's in the right."

Floyd let out a huff through his nose.

McCray looked back and forth from Daddy to Floyd. I could tell he was straining to not say anything more. Finally, he turned around and walked toward the trees on the far side of the path. He stood there, his back to us.

"Any luck?" Daddy asked Jonathan.

Jonathan shook his head. "I lost their tracks. Looks like they kept going up the trail."

“Damn it,” said Daddy. “Maybe we’ll find them along the way.”

Mama looked at Daddy, her chin resting on the part in Chenona’s black hair. “Are you sure you should be the one to go with Ahote?”

Daddy nodded. “Yes.”

That was all he said, and Mama didn’t ask anything else.

Daddy turned to Lenora and me. He nodded toward the woods and started walking.

“Come on,” said Lenora.

We caught up to him just as he reached the other end of the wagon. He turned to us, leaning his hip against the wheel.

“You’re leaving, Daddy?” Lenora asked.

He nodded. “I have to.”

“It doesn’t have to be you,” she said.

“It does and you know it. I can’t send McCray. Ahote would probably kill him before they walked a mile. And Floyd? Well . . . ”

Though Daddy didn’t finish the statement, I knew what he was going to say. Floyd wouldn’t make it. He wasn’t a tenderfoot or anything like that, but he wouldn’t last out there. Daddy was the only one, other than Ahote, who could endure a trek like that. And Ahote shouldn’t go alone.

“Then send Jonathan,” I said. “He can go with Ahote.”

Daddy shook his head. “Floyd would never allow that. Jonathan may be older, but he is still Floyd and Patty’s son. If they said no, which they would, then it would have to be that way.”

I knew Daddy was right. I didn’t like it, but there was no other way.

Daddy let out a breath that rattled his bearded cheeks. “There must be some civilization along the way somewhere. Hopefully, we’ll run across the horses. Either way, we’ll get some help, come back for the rest of you in a few days. That baby needs a doctor and, before long, more of us will need one, too.”

Daddy looked down at me. His eyes were the color of the snow. His hair dangled from under his hat, hanging in his eyes. I noticed there was gray in it that hadn’t been there when we’d left home. I realized that he looked ten years older.

“Billy,” he said. “You’re the man while I’m gone.”

Lenora snickered.

Daddy looked at her. “I’m serious. In my eyes, Lenora, you’re in charge, but Billy needs to be treated like a man and not a child. He will have to help you and your mother. Jonathan can’t do it all. James won’t be of much help, you both know that. That’s why I need Billy to be grown, even if for a little while. James can’t. He’ll be too much of a nuisance. Don’t you be one, too.”

“I won’t,” I said.

“Promise me.”

“I promise.”

Daddy held out his hand. I looked at it for a moment. Never had he offered to shake my hand before now. I reached out and put my hand against his. Though I was supposed to be a man, my hand was minuscule compared to his. His grip was strong and rough. When he shook his arm, my whole body twitched and jerked.

I wanted to hug him but wasn’t sure if that was something a man would do or not. Looking back on it now, I should have wrapped my arms around his waist and begged him not to go.

While Daddy and Ahote finished packing up, Jonathan brought more sticks from the woods, stacking them near the fire so they could thaw. One by one, he placed them in the fire. After a few minutes, they finally began to burn.

The men dragged out all the guns we had with us: two double-barrels, some rifles, and a few pistols. Sounds like a lot, I know, but really it wasn't. A shotgun and rifle each would be leaving with Daddy and Ahote, plus a pistol each. That was six guns that would be gone, leaving a rifle, shotgun, and two pistols for the group.

It was finally time for them to go.

Daddy came over and wrapped his big arms around Mama, Lenora, and me. He took turns hugging us, spending longer with Mama while whispering in her ear. She began to cry. I had never seen her cry before. It made me feel a little sick. What really surprised me was the tear I saw break loose from Daddy's eye. It ran down his cheek, turning to frost when it reached his beard.

Floyd had us all gather in a circle and pray before they left. It was a long prayer that I wasn't sure would ever end. When it finally did, Daddy and Ahote headed for the trail, bundled up and carrying very little. They waved to us all, then turned and started walking while the rest of us gave them our blessings.

They vanished in the shadowy conduit of the trail as if absorbed by the darkness.

We all continued to watch until one by one, we broke away.

I stood there the longest, staring at the darkness filling the trees, and I had never felt so alone in all my young life.

I said another prayer to God, a much shorter one than Floyd had done. It was simple.

I asked Him to protect Daddy and Ahote on their journey and to look out for us. For the first time, a peace seemed to trickle through me.

I told myself everything would be fine.

An hour later, snow began to fall.

5

IT WAS STILL SNOWING.

Daddy and Ahote had been gone for two days, and the sky hadn't stopped dropping fluffy pellets since the morning they walked away. It had piled high all around, forcing the skeletal tree limbs to bend downward. Sometimes, they'd sound like a rifle blast when they cracked and scared all of us. More than once, somebody cried out.

Sitting on my knees inside the wagon, I poked out my head between the flaps. The air smelled sweet. I stuck out my tongue, catching a couple flakes.

I looked over at Daddy's sleeping hut. It was empty. I don't know if I expected to see his boots jutting from the front, but I felt a sense of loss when I didn't see them. Dead branches and brown soggy leaves protruded from the snow that had collected overnight.

Floyd stood beside his tent, brushing off the snow. As quickly as he had it cleared, more had already began to recover it. Seeing this, he let out a grunt and swiped his hand through the air as if it might knock the snow away.

Mama was on her knees by the fire circle trying to light it with a match.

"You need something dry," said McCray, standing off to the side puffing a cigar. When he exhaled, he was swarmed by smoke.

"I don't have anything dry."

"Use this," said Patty. She handed Mama some paper. "I don't have much, so use it sparingly."

"Thank you," Mama said.

With the paper, Mama was able to get the fire to going. She added some more sticks, and the fire really took on.

"You're awake?" James asked behind me.

I turned around and saw he was sitting up, rubbing his head. He began to shiver. "Why's it so damn cold?"

"It's snowing again."

James groaned. "Snowing still, you mean. It hasn't stopped."

"It wasn't snowing when we turned in."

Ellie, lying between Lenora and Janey, began to move. The stirring seemed to wake up Lenora. She raised her head and looked around.

Jonathan, Chenona, and her baby were nowhere around.

"What'd you say?" asked Ellie.

"It's snowing," I said.

Last night, there'd been a break in the clouds. Just enough to let silver light spill down and wash the camp in a meager glow. Jack McCray had announced the worst of the weather was over. The fresh snow proved how little McCray knew about such things.

Lenora sat up. "How much snow?" She shuddered, rubbed her hands together.

"Fell all night, it looks. Still is."

Worry flashed across her face. I figured she was anxious about Daddy walking around out there. I was, too.

James sniffed. "I smell ham."

I could smell it, too. My stomach grumbled so much it hurt. For the last few days, there had been this cramp in my gut that wouldn't go away. Each day, it seemed a little worse than before. It wasn't unbearable or anything, but I feared at the rate it was increasing, it soon would be.

"Everyone bundle up," said Lenora. She shook Janey awake. "Time to wake up."

"Why?" asked Janey. "There's no sense going out there."

"Breakfast is cooking," said Lenora.

"Our small ration?"

"It's better than nothing at all," said Lenora. "Be grateful there's at least that much."

"Grateful," James muttered.

"You should all be grateful," said Lenora in a shaky voice.

James sighed. "Grateful for a slow death?"

"James!" said Janey through a gasp. "Shut your mouth."

"I'm just saying what's on everyone's minds. There's no hope. They're just pretending as if there is. We're doomed."

"Be quiet," I said. "That kind of talk won't do anybody any good."

"Oh, Billy's getting big for his britches, I see. Want me to pound you until you fit those britches again?"

"You do," said Lenora, "and you'll have to answer to me."

James looked at her. He smirked, shook his head. "You ain't all there."

"Apologize," said Lenora.

James let out a breath that puffed his pudgy cheeks. It filled the wagon with a nasty odor. "Sorry, Billy. Really. Shouldn't take it out on you."

"Fine," I said.

No one said anything for a few seconds.

Then Lenora said, "Everyone up. Let's go do our business so we can eat."

Janey sat up, moving like a child told she couldn't play with the other kids. Like the rest of us, she still wore her heavy coat. She grabbed her scarf and tied it around her neck and didn't stop wrapping until half her face was covered.

I understood her and James's frustrations. We were all used to eating regularly—three times a day, big meals that held us over until the next one. Water was aplenty, as was milk and coffee and sometimes juice.

"Where's Jonathan?" Janey asked.

"Still hunting," said Lenora. "I imagine he'll smell the food and come along soon enough."

Janey nodded.

"Chenona's gone," I said. "The baby, too."

"She'll be back," said Lenora. "She's probably praying. The baby is very sick. This weather and conditions . . . " She shook her head.

"That is *not* praying," said Janey. "What she does, the chanting and dancing around, is frightening. The other night, she rubbed this black stuff on her face. I saw her when I went to . . . " She didn't want to say take a shit, so she stopped talking.

"That *is* praying," said James. "Just the way her

people do it. It's like warpaint. A sign of respect. They taught us that at school. Their way of being holy."

"That doesn't sound holy to me," said Janey. "She looks like a damn devil when she does that."

"Enough," said Lenora. "Chenona was raised with ancient beliefs that we can't even begin to try to understand. Show her respect and give her privacy."

"Someone needs to put a Bible in her hand," said Janey.

"We can do that when we get to Harvest Hill." Lenora put on a polite smile that lacked the radiance it had possessed when we were still back at home.

Janey snorted. I wasn't sure if she snorted at the idea of giving Chenona a Bible and convincing her to deny centuries of Indian antiquity, or if it was the idea we would ever make it to Harvest Hill. I figured it was a little of both.

After we were all covered up, we climbed out of the wagon. James and I broke away from the girls and headed to the far side trees. The girls went another direction.

"Good morning," said Mama as we passed her. There were small pink wedges slowly sizzling on the pan. It smelled wonderful.

We told her the same, then entered the woods.

A few feet in, James and I stood with our backs together, pissing on the snow. My piss cut lines through the white. I tried to make shapes with them but couldn't stop shivering enough to do it.

"Have you ever wanted to sneak over and watch the girls piss?"

James' sudden question was so bizarre I couldn't answer right away. "Are you serious?"

"I'm not saying I would do it," said James. "I just wonder how they do it."

"You should know that already. Hell, I do and I'm only eleven."

"I know how it works. I wonder how *they* do it. Do they strip down? Just hike up the dresses and squat? How?"

"Those are our sisters. That's wrong."

"Ellie's not. She's pretty, too."

An image of Ellie crouched in the snow began to form in my mind, but I shook my head to kill it. "Shut up."

I finished and adjusted my pants. James was still going.

"Afraid my pecker might freeze and break before I finish," said James.

"I'm heading back," I said.

"Hold on, I'm done."

I heard the whispery rustles of his clothes, then James stepped up beside me. He wasn't much taller than me, but he was at least two widths of me wide. His face was pink under his hat, his cheeks dotted with purple blotches. Somehow, even in these cold temperatures he was sweating.

We made our way back to the camp. The girls were already there. Everyone had sat down around the fire on our various logs.

I could smell bacon and coffee.

Mama held the pan by its handle, using a cloth to protect her skin from burns. "Enjoy this. It was the last of the ham. We're almost out of coffee too."

"Son of a bitch," muttered McCray.

Mary whispered something to him. He acted as if

she hadn't spoken at all. The hair on his face was grimy with snow and ice, but I could see the anger as if he were clean-shaved.

Mama served us. She made sure to save a little for Chenona and Jonathan. Nobody spoke while we ate.

Jonathan returned a short while later. We were all glad to see him until we saw he only carried his rifle with him.

He hadn't shot anything.

6

WE ATE POTATOES for breakfast the next morning. There was barely enough to split between us, and we had to leave enough for supper, too. The adults had decided we would only eat twice a day to try and save as much as we could.

Over the days that followed, Chenona barely ate at all. She would nibble, then retreat to the wagon with her baby. When she wasn't in there, she would go to the woods and come back much later. Mama told her she needed to eat. The baby needed to be nurtured, and there wouldn't be anything to suckle if Chenona didn't eat.

But Chenona continued doing what she was doing. After a while, she no longer spoke to us. Nobody tried to speak to her, either.

One day, Mama found some jerky that Daddy had stowed away in the wagon. There was enough we were able to spread it out over two nights.

We tried to ration the supplies as much as we could. But there were many of us. Nowhere near enough to go around. And we were hungry.

Then there was nothing left but beans.

No coffee.

No meat.

No vegetables.

Then there were no beans.

Only snow. There was plenty of snow and ice.

Snow that would stop falling for a day, only to start up again the next even heavier. Floyd Shumaker liked to remark that he'd never seen it snow like this in all his days. When McCray told him to not to say it again, I was grateful.

Thought about telling Lenora I was finally grateful for something.

When Daddy left, I promised myself I would count the days until he returned with help.

Then I stopped because it made me sad. I began to realize he probably wasn't coming back. He hadn't abandoned us. I figured he just never made it out of the woods. Realizing that filled me with a deep sadness that caused my muscles to feel leaden.

Nights, I buried my face in the blanket and quietly sobbed. I strained to hold my body still so nobody would feel me jerking. But the sobs were heavy and always left me feeling weak and tired when they passed. I figured if anyone ever asked, I could tell them I was just cold. They'd believe that because we all fell asleep trembling. The little I did sleep I would dream that Daddy came back with a rescue party. We would hug and there would be food.

When I woke up and understood it was all just a dream, I would cry more.

Then I decided sleep wasn't worth the sorrow my dreams brought and started staying awake until my body forced my mind into a deep slumber. If I dreamed then, I surely don't remember it.

Those nights, I listened to the wind howl outside,

the flutter and flaps of the hammercloth. At times, it would beat the fabric so hard I thought it might rip it clear off. Everyone else slept. Sometimes, Mama would whimper in her sleep, but other than that it was silent.

Even the baby had stopped waking up in the middle of the night.

That worried me. I didn't know much about babies, but I knew enough that babies didn't sleep through the night as much as Chenona's did. I also knew that babies didn't sleep most of the day like Chenona's did.

And I realized in those long nights, that I didn't even know what the baby's name was. Maybe he didn't have one. I used to hear stories that Indian men had to earn their names. But Ahote was an Indian trying to divorce himself from that culture, so it was odd that he would keep that tradition.

Maybe I just hadn't been paying attention.

Another dawn came. Which number it was, I have no clue. They all began to blur together into a never-ending loop, almost repeating with only the accumulation of more misery to separate them from each other.

I looked around. The inside of the wagon was filling with grey light. I must have dozed for a little while.

Chenona was gone again.

More snow had fallen during the night, but there was a break the next morning.

We drank hot water we'd made from melting the snow and boiling it over the fire. There was a creek, but it was too far of a hike to do every day. Jonathan had discovered it during one of his hunts that had produced nothing for us.

We didn't talk while we sipped warm water. It burned my throat going down and spread fire in my belly. Though there was no taste, nor did it quench my thirst, it filled me with warmth.

I watched the others. It was hard to ignore the grim mood that felt like an invisible web we were all stuck in. Remembering how fresh and eager we all looked when we started our journey, seeing us now was like looking at a party of living corpses.

There was barely any movement. We were clothed in filthy rags, wrapped upon layers of other tatters. Only our faces were exposed, and those had become patched in frost with cracked lips that glistened under crispy blood.

I prayed to God to either save us or kill us. Torturing us like this was cruel. I wondered what we'd done to be punished in such a way.

Mama looked over her shoulder.

"Nobody's coming," muttered McCray

"I was looking for Chenona."

Patty turned to look as well. "She's off doing whatever it is she does."

"Let her be gone," said McCray. "The less I see of her, the better."

Mary nudged his arm with her elbow. McCray harrumphed but said no more.

After we finished our water, the mothers gathered the wood we'd brought in last night so it could thaw.

McCray suggested all the men should go hunting this time. More eyes searching for food wouldn't hurt.

We split into groups. McCray and Floyd went one

direction into the woods, and James and I joined Jonathan going the other way.

We walked close together, looking this way and that. The woods were still, as if it were holding its breath until we passed by. Far in the distance, I could hear the shrill whistling of a wind we couldn't feel where we were.

"I'm tired," said James.

"Hush," said Jonathan.

"Can we rest a minute?"

"No."

"Please?"

Jonathan sighed. "Good way to let the critters know we're hunting 'em is talking."

"You been out here alone talkin' to nobody and still ain't shot a thing."

I felt a snicker rise in my throat, but it was too dry to produce a sound.

"Fine," said Jonathan.

We approached a felled tree. Sharp blades of wood jutted from the stump. It had turned a dull grey hue.

"Careful," said Jonathan, pointing at the stump.

We made our way around it and plopped down on the tree. It felt good to be off my feet. Though it was freezing outside, I was sweating underneath the tiers of clothes.

I turned and caught Jonathan staring at me. I felt a pulse of heat work through me.

"You doin' all right?" he asked.

I nodded. "Tired."

"You're not sleepin'. I hear you, you know."

My cheeks blazed. I wondered how much he had

heard, if he'd been awake those nights I'd lay there bawling.

James wrinkled his nose. "What's he doin' at night? Bad dreams?"

"Nothin'," I said.

"Why don't you talk to your ma about it?" he asked. "Or Lenora?"

"What's to say?"

"You're worried about your daddy, huh?"

"I bet he is," said James. "How long they been gone? Too damn long."

"Shut up, James," said Jonathan. "He knows all that."

I felt tears starting to burn my eyes.

Jonathan must have seen what his talk was doing to me. He nodded, then slid off the tree. His feet smacked the ground. "Well, I'm tired of babysittin' you two. I'm gonna go off that way." He pointed to the left. "You two go there." He pointed to the right.

"What are we supposed to do?" asked James. "Slay an animal with our bare hands?"

Jonathan reached into his coat and tugged out a pistol. I recognized it right away. It was Daddy's Colt.

Gasping, James reached for the pistol. Jonathan shoved his hand away.

"Hey," said James, looking at his brother as if he'd spit in his eye.

"This ain't for you."

"Where'd you get that?" I asked. "That's my daddy's."

"He left it with Lenora. She's lettin' me use it."

I didn't like that Lenora had it and didn't tell me. But I liked it even less that she was letting Jonathan traipse all over the woods with one of Daddy's guns. I decided not to worry about too much.

"Billy keeps the gun," said Jonathan.

"What?" said James, his squeaky voice slicing through the air. "I'm three years older!"

"Yes, and he's a better shot than you are. So he keeps the gun." Holding it by the barrel, Jonathan offered me the Colt.

I struggled to keep my hands from shaking as I reached for it. I'd never shot the Colt before. I recognized the tobacco leaf engraved in the handle and felt my throat go tight.

It felt heavy in my hand. Good, natural, but heavy. I wondered how hard it would kick when it was fired.

"He can't hit any birds with that," said James. "What if we see birds?"

"You couldn't hit the broad side of a bear if you saw one. But I bet he could. I bet he could drop a dove with one shot clipping its wing. I've seen him shoot. He's that good."

I hoped the redness from the cold would hide how hard my cheeks were burning. I used my free hand to adjust the scarf Mama had tied around me, hiking it up to hide the lower half of my face.

Jonathan was right, though. I was pretty good shot. It was something that I hadn't even had to work at. The first time Daddy had put a rifle in my hand, I blew a hole through a playing card pinned to a tree. From then on, Daddy had taken me shooting often. He used to kid around with me and make me swear I'd never run off and join an outlaw gang because of my skills.

"You can handle that, right?" Jonathan asked. He was looking right at me. His dark eyes were serious.

I nodded. “Think so.”

“You have to know,” said Jonathan. “That beauty has a kickback on her that could shatter your nose if you’re not ready for it.”

I held the gun up, staring at the barrel. It offered a smeared blot of myself as a reflection. I smiled behind the scarf. “Bet your ass I can handle it.”

Jonathan chuckled. “That’s what I want to hear. And I won’t tell your mama you cursed like that, either.”

“Thank you.”

“Be careful, you two. Try to find us something to eat. We can’t go another day on hot water. We’ve been in trouble for a while, but now it’s critical.”

Jonathan’s words turned my momentary good mood sour. I nodded. “I know.”

Jonathan patted James on the shoulder. “You boys be careful. Got your watches?”

“No,” said James.

“I have mine,” I said, patting my pocket. I couldn’t feel it under the heavy layers, but I knew it was there. Daddy had given it to me last year for Christmas. I always had it on me.

“Good. Meet me back here in one hour. I hope to hell one of us has something.”

Before we could say anything else, Jonathan turned and rushed toward a patch of trees. He stepped around them and was swallowed by brown and white.

“What the hell are we supposed to do now?” asked James.

“Find us some food.”

James snorted.

We turned and started walking. I had no idea where we should go, so I just walked. James stayed with me, not disputing my sporadic choices in direction.

"Do you think we're going to die out here?"

James's question caused my throat to close. I struggled to swallow. "I hope not."

"Well, I hope not, too. I didn't ask what you hoped for. I asked if you think we're going to."

I saw myself on my back in the wagon, lying on those thin sheets with the hard, unyielding wood under me. I figured that was where it would happen if it did happen. I'd be in that cold, dark womb, surrounded by people but somehow alone.

Would I go peacefully in my sleep, or would it hurt?

I didn't want to think about it. "No," I said. "We're going to be all right."

"You're a damn liar, Billy Coburn. A shit liar, at that."

I shrugged my shoulders. "What's it help if I say we *are* going to die? Nothing."

"But you think we are. Like I think so."

"I'm not answering that. You remember Lenora that day. Be grateful."

"Grateful for what? That we're slowly dying? You know we are, don't you? Dying? We been doing that since that first horse dropped dead. Maybe I should get on my knees and thank our merciless God for blessing us with such a pitiful death."

I wanted to slug him. Not only was I too small to do any damage other than pissing him off, I was also way too tired to fret with trying. Made me uncomfortable when people spoke ill of the Lord. I wasn't sure how much I believed in what the Bible said, but I guess I believed enough to not like slander.

Still, he was right. I knew it. He knew it. But talking about it wouldn't help the situation feel any less awful than it already did.

"What's that?" asked James. "Tracks?"

James had turned his head slightly to the left. I looked. At first, I didn't see anything but snow and trees. There were some broken limbs scattered here and there, protruding from the snow like wooden arms. Then I saw them—a trail of depressions in the snow leading away from us. From where I stood, they looked medium-sized and oval-shaped.

They looked fresh.

I held up the pistol.

"Looks pretty big," said James in a quieter voice. "Think it's coyote?"

The tracks weren't huge, but they were definitely larger than a mutt's. I didn't think they belonged to anything as big as a bear, either. "Could be a deer," I said, though I didn't really think so. Unless it was a large deer, bigger than I'd ever seen.

We slowed our walk, easing our feet onto the snow with each step. The snow shifted under my boots with a quiet squish sound.

We reached the tracks and my excitement turned to confusion.

The tracks were human.

Pairs of bare footprints cut a path in the snow.

James started following them before I even had a chance to stop him.

"James," I said, my voice low. "Don't."

He either didn't hear me or chose to ignore me. I hurried to catch up. We walked alongside the tracks, following them around a large tree that was missing most of its bark.

James jerked to a halt.

I bumped into him, nearly dropping the pistol. "Why'd you stop . . . ?"

James lifted his arm, pointing a trembling finger. I had to step around his mass to see what he was showing me.

When I did, my mouth dropped open.

It was Chenona. She stood in a rock circle about as wide as two wagon wheels, facing away from us. Naked, her dark skin was slick and shiny. Her hair was a black mane down between her shoulder blades. Head tilted back, she spoke in her native language at the sky as her body shook.

My penis stiffened. The cold made the act painful.

Her arms were raised, straight and wide in a Y shape. Her fingers were extended, hands twitching as she chanted. The backs of her legs tensed, her buttocks cluenched.

I noticed James was making shrill breathy noises.

I felt sick watching her like this, invading her private moment. But I couldn't stop looking. I didn't want to stop looking and that made me feel even worse. I don't even think I blinked while leering at the way her muscles undulated under her smooth skin.

Tearing my eyes away was harder than I would have thought. I aimed them to the right of her.

And that was when I saw the baby.

He was supine on a blanket, naked. His skin was not the same supernatural darkness of his mother.

His skin was purple.

Good God, I thought. The baby's dead.

7

THE INFANT'S EYES were dull slits on a face that was a prune hue. Its mouth, a small oval, looked frozen in place, as if he'd passed while yawning.

I'd felt sick watching Chenona without her clothes on. Seeing her dead baby, I felt as if I might die myself.

Chenona started to turn around.

I felt a tug on my shoulder, then I was yanked to the ground behind a bush. I started to say something, but James's hand covered my mouth. He shushed me in the ear.

"She can't know we saw her," he whispered.

I nodded. He was right. I wished we hadn't come this way. I wished we hadn't stumbled upon Chenona doing her incongruous prayer ritual. I'd acted like a peeper, spying on her during a private occurrence just so I could get a glimpse of her naked bits.

I got more than I ever expected to.

And I felt lousy.

James moved his hand away from my mouth.

"Who's there?"

I froze at the sound of Chenona's voice. How did she know we were there? There was no way she could see through all the brush and snow. Then I saw my breath in front of me, floating up in wavy clouds.

"Shit," I muttered. "She can see our breath."

James's pale face seemed to dip two more shades. He covered his own mouth this time. I did the same. It stifled our puffs of air but did not stop them completely.

"Who *is* there?" Chenona asked again.

I heard the soft crunches of her feet on the snow, followed by the rustling of fabric. She was getting dressed.

"What is this?" McCray's voice.

I heard footsteps. Sounded like more than one pair, which meant Floyd Shumaker was still with him.

"Leave me," she said. "This is my moment with my deceased."

"The baby . . . ?" Floyd's voice petered out, unable to finish the sentence. "Jesus. Chenona, I'm so sorry."

"My baby is with the spirits. I must finish or . . . "

"When did this happen?" asked McCray. There was no concern or even sympathy in his voice. He asked as if she had accidentally broken something valuable.

"During the night," she said, her voice growing thick. "Please, leave me."

"Come on, Jack," said Floyd. "She's mourning. We're interrupting . . . "

"Shut up, Floyd."

Silence.

I stared at James, who stared at me, while we waited for the talking to continue. I could tell the silence was not good. It meant people were thinking. It meant *McCray* was thinking. I'd learned enough about him in the weeks we'd been traveling that whenever his mind got to working, it wasn't good.

Finally, he spoke, "What are you planning to do with the baby?"

"Bury him."

"You have no tools."

"I am not intended to use tools. My hands are my tools."

"You'll hurt yourself," said Floyd. There was disgust in his voice. "You'll tear your hands to pieces trying to dig that way. Let's get a shovel and do this proper—"

"This is how it is supposed to be. My blood will be in the dirt with him. A part of me will be with him eternally. Now, please, go."

"That's not a proper burial," said McCray. "Not for a child."

"It is my way," said Chenona. "My people's way."

"Your people's way is blasphemous. It disgusts me. You disgust me."

"I am not fond of you, either, Jack McCray."

McCray muttered something I couldn't understand.

"Come on, Jack," said Floyd, interrupting him. "We should go. She needs to be alone."

"She's gonna damn freeze to death."

"Not our concern," said Floyd. "Let's go."

After a moment, McCray said, "Yeah. This makes me want to vomit the air in my belly."

The crunches of their footfalls grew louder as they neared the bush. I knew any moment they would step around the side of the shrubs and catch us there. But they turned before going that far.

The crunching sounds of their boots faded as they kept going. Soon, I couldn't hear them at all.

After a short while, Chenona began to chant again. Her strange sounds blended with the scrapes and scratches of digging.

I began to lift my head. James slapped his hand down on my shoulder. He shook his head. I pulled away and continued to rise. My eyes scanned the shrubs then rose above them. Chenona, naked and on all fours, clawed at the ground. She'd peeled away layers of snow and was working at the frozen ground underneath.

Her dark hair hung over her face like a veil, blocking her vision of us. Her large breasts swayed over the ground, her nipples cutting into the snow.

I dropped back down. "Let's get back," I said in a low whisper.

James nodded. Then we crawled away from the wall of shrubs. When we were a good distance from it and could barely hear the chanting, we jumped to our feet and ran.

We didn't stop until we dashed out of the woods, kicking up snow behind us. Mama was there, crouched over the fire. She held a small bundle of sticks as if she were about to drop them on.

"What happened?" Her eyes lowered to the pistol in my hand.

We stopped running. James leaned over, gasping. He couldn't catch his breath to speak at all.

I said, "Nothing happened."

She tilted her face. She studied me. "Are you lying to me, William Coburn?"

I shook my head. "No ma'am."

"Then why were you running?"

I wasn't sure what to say. I opened my mouth, hoping an excuse would just come out on its own.

Then I spotted McCray standing over by the wagon. His eyes caught mine. I wondered if he knew we were there, listening. I didn't think he had any proof, but I was certain he suspected something was amiss.

I looked at mother and put on an expression that I hoped passed for humiliation. "We were just seeing who was faster."

"What? A race?"

I nodded. "Yes ma'am."

Mama looked at James. "Is this true?"

James nodded behind a cloud of fog puffing from his mouth. "It's . . . true."

Though I could tell she thought we were lying, she turned away and began adding the sticks to the fire. "I take it you didn't shoot anything? Or each other?"

James and I both started to answer. I paused, giving him the opportunity to finish, but he also paused. I went to answer when I guessed he decided to as well and we just ended up talking all over each other again.

Finally, James shut up and I said, "No. Didn't shoot anything."

"That's your daddy's gun." She looked at it, her eyes washing over with loss. She bit down on her bottom lip.

I worried she might start crying. She looked away before she could and resumed tending to the fire. James and I stood there another minute or so, then decided she was through talking with us.

We walked over to the wagon. I looked inside. Lenora was in there, cocooned in a thick blanket. Janey and Ellie sat in front of her, huddled close under a thick layer of blankets. Lenora held the Bible in her hand, reading. I recognized the verse from Genesis.

A lone candle burned, fixed in place on the wood floor in a cradle of melted candlewax. The flame painted the interior in a piss glow.

She saw us, lowered the thick book. Her face was pale around the dark circles for her eyes and mouth the shadows caused. “Any success?”

I shook my head.

Her shoulders sagged. The book drooped lower on her lap. She quickly shook it off and began to raise the book again. She caught sight of me and paused. “Are you okay?”

I looked over at James, then back at her. Though I said, “Fine,” I shook my head to indicate nothing was fine at all. She must have picked up on it because she continued to stare at me. “Janey, keep going where I left off.”

Janey groaned. “I don’t want to read.”

“Do it. Ellie is enjoying it.”

Ellie shook her head. “I’m not really—”

“Just read it,” said Lenora. “James, get in here and listen. It’s your lesson for the day. When I get back, we’re going to discuss the language and the meanings behind the Word.”

James let his head sag. “Why? What’s the point? And Billy’s not . . . ”

“I need to talk to him.”

James looked at me. His eyes were wide. I saw the words he wanted to say behind the panicked gawk.

Don’t tell her!

I shook my head. He seemed to understand that I was promising him I wouldn’t. I saw a mask of relief come over him.

8

"ARE YOU SURE the baby was dead?" Lenora asked.

We were walking along the path we'd taken in here. Our wagon tracks had long since been covered with snow. There was no indication anybody had traveled through there at all.

We walked the same pace, sharing her wool blanket as if we were one giant person. She held it in place in front of us so only our faces were exposed. Though I was a few years younger, I was nearly her height.

I nodded. "Very sure. I've never seen a fresh dead person, but I know what a living one looks like, and that baby did not look alive. It was like at Grandpappy's funeral, where he was all done up in that color on his face. The baby was only one color—purple. Dark purple. All over."

Shivering, Lenora pulled the blanket tighter around us. "This isn't good."

"I know."

"Soon as word gets out Chenona's baby is dead, all hope will be lost."

"Hasn't it been lost already?"

"No. Look at us. We're still working at it. Every

day, Jonathan hunts for food. One day, he'll find some. Whether it's just a tiny squirrel or a fat deer, he'll find us something."

"You really believe that, don't you?"

"I believe in God. I believe He won't let us starve to death. We have done nothing wrong."

"But don't wrong things happen to folks who haven't done no wrongs all the time?"

I looked over at my sister. Her lips had pressed to form a tight line. When she opened her mouth, her lips took a moment to stretch back out. "Doesn't mean God's the one causing it. Sure, wrongs happen all the time. Sometimes, nobody deserves what they get. Other times, people who don't deserve tons of good get it all. But that don't mean God's up there making it rough on us. We're in a bad spot. God knows it. God will see us through. You wait and see."

In that moment, I wanted to share my sister's faith. She was strong in it. I barely acknowledged prayer or faith of any kind, unless I was in some kind of trouble. Whenever I'd messed up and knew some kind of strict punishment would be coming my way, I dropped to my knees and prayed for a way out. Never was I granted that reprieve, but I suppose it was because I deserved what was coming to me.

But I also knew we were in the *worst* kind of trouble. I doubted any of us had been anywhere close to a dire situation like this in all our lives. Why weren't all of us gathered together in constant prayer? Why weren't we on our knees from sunup to sundown, calling on God to pull us out of this suffering. If he loves us so much, wouldn't he be happy to save us?

Because nobody truly believed in all that gospel shit. Not even Mama, or Daddy. Not even the Shumakers and definitely not the McCrays. Only Lenora did. Even now, in my senior years, I can't bring myself to accept it.

I sighed. "Do you think Daddy's alive?"

"I think he would never stop trying to help us, no matter what."

That didn't answer my question at all. But I understood it would be the only answer I'd get.

"So what are we going to do?" I asked.

"We keep the business about Chenona's baby to ourselves. Nobody needs to know that y'all saw what happened out there between her and Mr. McCray and Mr. Shumaker. You did right by not running in blabbing about it. Just need to make sure James doesn't go shootin' off his trap and telling everybody."

"I don't reckon he will. He told me not to say anything to anybody, even you."

"Good. That boy likes to run his mouth something fierce."

"Doesn't feel right. I feel . . . " I wasn't sure how I felt, really.

"I know." Lenora stopped walking. She turned to face me. She only had to look down a little to see me. "You're growing up. You're going to find yourself in lots of instances that don't make no sense. You'll soon realize how much better it was to be young and not know how things really are. Once you find out how the world really is, you'll hardly ever find a moment of joy."

"Is that what happened to you?"

Lenora's mouth dropped open. "William Coburn, how dare you?"

My cheeks heated. "I didn't mean it that way. I mean . . . "

"Do tell, Billy. What *do* you mean?" I saw the corner of her mouth arcing upward.

"You always seem like you're worrying about something. You don't smile so much. Is that what you mean will happen to me also?"

Lenora's nose wrinkled. "Maybe not. I always have a lot on my mind. Somebody's always tryin' to get at me, from the boys and men in town, to Mama nagging me about marriage plans. And that doesn't even begin to tell the strain Jonathan brings me. He means well, he does, but he just always seems to be planning things for me without my involvement at all."

I knew what she meant by all that. I'd witnessed it myself.

"But as you get older, you begin to realize there's not a lot to smile about anymore."

"Wonderful. Hopefully I never turn into somebody like Mr. McCray."

Lenora laughed. It was good to hear, a chortle that split through the cold and reminded me of what things were like only a month ago. "You ever show any hints of being like that cold-hearted dung-pile, I'll whip you myself."

I could tell she meant it, and I'm not ashamed to admit a tingle of fear grabbed at me.

"Come on," Lenora said. "Let's make our way back." She looked up. "Hasn't snowed all day. Maybe that's a good sign this winter weather will leave us be for a spell."

"I hope so."

"Me too."

We started back to camp.

By the time we reached it, droplets of snow were starting to drift down.

9

WE TURNED IN EARLY. I resumed my position in the far corner of the wagon by the rear. Buried under the blankets, I stared at the pale ceiling while listening to Lenora read to us by candlelight. She kept yawning through the passages, so Jonathan took over for her so she could lie down.

I liked the way he read the stories. He used different voices and really articulated a performance, unlike Lenora who read like she was speaking her final rites before an execution.

I found myself really enjoying it. I began to distance myself from the morning, from the sight of the dead baby. I began to forget about McCray and Floyd's confrontation with Chenona.

In fact, it was pretty easy to forget all about them since I rarely saw the two men all day. Only their wives were any indication the men had been nearby. Patty and Mary had been scurrying about all day as if working on something.

Lenora had asked Mama what they were up to, but Mama only shook her head and told us not to fret over them none. So I didn't. I was just glad to be rid of them all, even if for only a day. It made our condition a tad more tolerable without their constant complaining and fighting.

Plus, McCray's presence seemed to suck what little life remained from all of us. I felt livelier, damn near a good mood for somebody who was slowly starving to death.

Like Chenona, the men weren't at camp when we retired. Jonathan wanted James and I to join him before the first crack of dawn. He felt an earlier start on the day might benefit us more in our hunt. I didn't agree, but it was something to focus on, and I would get to leave camp again.

Maybe that's why I was able to drift off to sleep. I hadn't forgotten everything that happened that day, but I had been able to sort of shove it to the back of my mind and pin it there. The exhaustion and fatigue from hunger might have had something to do with it, but either way, I was glad to sleep that night.

When I awoke, it was still dark. Jonathan was no longer reading. The wagon was filled with a mishmash of breathing and snores. I knew right away Mama, Patty, and Mary weren't among them. It was quieter without their breathing, and there seemed to be a lot more space inside. They'd still been up when we'd turned in, but that was not unusual. They normally came in the wagon shortly after us.

But this time they hadn't. I was sure of it.

I sat up. The blanket fell away from me and it suddenly felt as if I was clutched in a frigid hand. I pulled the covering back up, holding it at my throat with one hand while reaching for the cloth with the other.

I pulled it open and peered out.

The fire had dwindled to embers. Faint red glowed inside the charred pile as if a fiendish spirit might dwell underneath. I saw nobody, only the small shelters Floyd and McCray had been sleeping in. They were dark shapes against the night behind them. The snow seemed to spread a dull light throughout the area, making it easier for me to see that nobody was inside those tents.

Something was wrong.

I turned around. Though it was black as pitch inside the wagon, I knew where everyone was sleeping. Lenora was on the opposite end, next to an empty section where Mama would have been sleeping had she come in last night.

I wanted to wake her, but to do that I would have had to crawl over James, Jonathan, Janey, and Ellie to reach her. I'd wind up waking everyone. But I knew that would be the right decision just so I could have Lenora's help in this matter.

I was about to start making my way to her when I heard it, the soft crunching of footsteps in the snow. Somebody was moving quickly, yet with a calculated intent of being quiet. Whoever was out there was sneaking in a way not to rouse anyone.

I looked back through the small gap in the cloth.

And saw Mama.

Washed in a dim, gray glow, she came from the woods on the far side of camp, hunched over and hugging herself. She didn't have her blanket with her. She wore the thick dress she'd been wearing this whole time. Her hair was starting to droop from the pin she used to keep it huddled behind her head.

At first, I thought she was coming to the wagon.

She seemed to be heading straight toward it. Then she stopped by the spent fire. Crouching, she scooped up the stick bundle. They had been wrapped in burlap to keep the cold off.

Holding it to her bosom, she turned and rushed back to the woods. I watched her vanish in the inky black inside the trees.

What was she doing?

I decided I would wait to wake Lenora. I wanted to see what Mama was up to on my own.

Pulling on my boots, my hands shook from the cold and my nerves. The twisting in my stomach was painful, but the unease made it almost hard to move. A flurry of thoughts rushed through my head, all of them centered on Mama and why she had been acting so suspect. It took longer than it should have, but I got on my boots.

I crawled to the border of wood at the mouth of the wagon. I debated taking my blanket with me, but I decided to leave it behind. My coat would have to be enough.

Outside, the cold felt like frozen blades slicing at my face as I started walking toward the woods. The snow drifted down like bits of cotton, making soft plopping sounds when they struck me.

"Billy?"

I froze at the voice that came from behind me. It was barely above a whisper, just loud enough that I was able to detect it. I couldn't tell who it was from its hushed note. I figured it was probably Lenora, or maybe even James. Somebody had seen me climb out of the wagon.

Slowly, I turned around. Relief flowed through me

when I saw Ellie's head peeking out between the draping cloth. Her face looked pale except for the dark smudges the shadows made on her cheeks. Snow clung to the long hair curtaining the sides of her face.

"Where are you going?" she said.

I put my finger to my mouth. Then I pointed to the woods. Ellie looked as if she were about to say something, then thought better of it. Her head slipped back inside the curtain. It swayed before going still. I wasn't sure what she was doing. I kind of figured she was waking up Lenora and telling her she'd caught me trotting off into the woods at night.

When the curtain opened again, I expected to see my sister peering out at me. Instead, it was Ellie again. She swung a leg out over the jut of the frame and let it dangle. She must have been putting on her boots since she was now wearing them.

Keeping one foot balanced on the frame, she brought out the other one and let herself drop. Her feet hit the snow with a muffled thump, her body sinking to a crouch before straightening again. She turned and looked at me. Her smile seemed to spread light across her face.

I couldn't help but smile back.

She caught up to me, moving fast but making sure she was as quiet as possible. "What are you doing?" she asked when she reached me.

"I saw Mama."

Ellie's head tilted. "Out here?"

"A couple minutes ago. She sneaked in here and took our sticks."

Ellie turned to look, as if confirming my claim. Then she faced me again. "Why would she do that?"

I shrugged.

"Was my mother with her?"

I shook my head. "She was alone."

"So is that what you're up to? Sneaking off to see what she's doing?"

Hearing her say it made me feel like an ass. What did it matter what she was doing? She was the adult, and I was the kid. It was none of my business, and if she knew I was trying to be nosey about it, she was liable to tan my hide.

Still, something just was sitting right in my gut, and it wasn't just the hunger.

"I suppose I am," I said.

Ellie nodded. "I'll go with you."

I involuntarily shivered. Never had I been alone with Ellie before. And now we were about to walk off into the dark woods, just the two of us. I gripped my coat inside the pockets, trying to calm myself. I didn't trust myself to speak, so I nodded. Her smile returned, stretching wide on her face.

"Which way did she go?" Ellie asked.

I cleared my throat. "This way."

10.

MAMA'S TRACKS WERE black hollows in the snow. They led into the woods, vanishing inside the curtain of night on the other side of the trees. The darkness looked very dark over there, blacker than pitch. Ellie must have felt the same cringe of fear I did because she let out a shuddery breath.

"Well," Ellie said. "Guess we better get to it."

"Yep. Guess we better."

We continued to stand there, side by side, our elbows brushing together. I looked over at her and saw she was gazing up at me. I might have been a little less than two years younger than her, I was still a foot taller. I realized she was waiting on me to go first.

"All right," I said. "Let's go."

It took more effort than I thought to get my legs moving. The snow squished under my boots, shifting with each step. It wasn't hard to see, thanks to the stark white of the snow giving us enough illumination to avoid tree branches and jutting roots here and there.

We moved at a careful pace just the same, though. I wasn't taking any chances of tripping and hurting myself, or Ellie doing the same. How would we explain that the next day?

We'd been walking a little over ten minutes when I began to hear voices. The scent of woodsmoke drifted toward me, blended with a sweet smell that was so pungent it was almost sour.

Somehow, it smelled good and nauseated me all at once.

"Somebody's cookin'," Ellie said.

"It's meat," I said. I knew it for certain.

"Look. A fire."

I saw what Ellie was talking about—a flickering orange cast against the tops of the trees, wriggling to the rhythm of crackling wood. I no longer worried so much about being discreet because the fire noise would mask our movements.

"Come on," I said.

Walking at a brisk pace, we reached a pair of emaciated trees sheathed in ice. On the other side was the campfire. The radiance was brighter over there.

Ducking low, I scurried up to the tree with Ellie right beside me. Overhangs of bare branches scraped at the ground. Ellie pointed to the dark cave the branches created, then she hurried into the blackness. It looked as if she dived into a pool of black that swallowed her bit by bit. I felt a scurrying sensation on my spine. I didn't want go in there. It was too dark. Before I could dwell on it, Ellie's face reappeared, sticking out from the darkness. Her eyes were narrowed as she looked up at me.

I knew she was wondering what I was doing. Not wanting to look like a chicken in front of Ellie, I got on all fours. The snow soaked through my pants as I crawled into the darkness. Heavy shade fell over me, blotting out everything except for the fluttering orange on the other side of the branches. I felt there was enough shadow to conceal us, but enough room was left to see what was happening.

It was warmer here, close to the fire. The heat had caused some of the ice to melt. I felt drips on my shoulder from the limbs above me.

I didn't plan to stay long. Just enough to observe what they were up to, so I could go back and inform Lenora. I figured she and Jonathan would be in a better place to confront the adults than either Ellie or myself were in.

"Daddy," Ellie said in a shocked whisper.

Squatted beside the fire, McCray was turning a tree branch like a handle. My eyes moved to the left and saw another branch had been placed on top of two tethered branches implanted in the ground. It extended away from it, vanishing inside a hump of charred meat before reemerging on the other side and resting on a matching pair of crossed sticks.

I saw Mama off to the side, holding out the bundle of sticks to Mary.

"Thank you," said Mary. She took the bundle and unwrapped them like a gift.

"We have to be sure to replace them," said Mama. "If we don't . . . "

"We know," said Floyd Shumaker. He sat on the stump of a felled tree. Patty was on his lap, her pretty face washed in the flickering light. He held her close. "We will replace them. They won't know."

"We have to do it soon, so they can dry out by morning for the fire."

"Claire," said Mary. "Enough. You worrying is making me nervous."

Nodding, Mama turned to stare at the meat slowly churning. The flames licked the undersides of the lump. She nibbled at her bottom lip. I saw the lower tips of her top teeth. She looked nervous, though the hunger in her gaze seemed more prominent.

"They have food," said Ellie. I could see the faint smudges of her eyes in the darkness. The fire glistened in them, showing tears were forming. "Why would they hide that from us?" Her voice was rising.

I leaned forward, putting my hand to her mouth. She flinched at the coldness of my fingers. "Don't be so loud. If they catch us . . . "

Ellie nodded. She didn't need for me to finish the sentence. Together, we turned our attention back to the adults.

Mama was still pacing. Her feet had dug a small trench in the snow. "Doesn't anyone feel bad about this?" she asked.

McCray snorted.

"I mean . . . isn't this . . . ungodly?"

"We prayed," said McCray. "All of us. Together. Remember?"

Mama nodded. "Yes. We prayed for food."

"And the Lord provided."

"Are you sure this is what *He* provided? Or did we just take it out of greed?"

McCray stopped turning the makeshift spit and looked up at Mama. "At this point, Claire, what the hell does it matter? We're hungry. Damn-near starved, and this . . . " He held out his hands to the roasting meat. " . . . was right there. *Waiting* for us to take. Are we proud of ourselves? No. Do we like what we've had to resort to?"

"No," answered Mary, standing behind her husband. She put a hand on his shoulder. Her face was smudged in shadows.

"But are we going to turn our nose up to what has been provided?"

"Seems almost wrong if we don't do this," said Floyd.

Patty nodded. "Spitting in the face of God."

McCray shook his head. "Remember how all the people complained about what Moses did for them? Remember? God punished them with sour milk and bread. We will not make that mistake. This trial we've been in? We're going to get through it. If we have to do something we don't like to survive, then so be it. I will not be punished any longer."

Mama sighed. "But shouldn't we give it to the children? Aren't they the ones who need it the most?"

My stomach grumbled as if to agree with her.

Patty shook her head. "What good would it do if their bellies are full for a day while ours go hungry? How are we supposed to care for them if we're starved? Only Jonathan and Lenora are even of age to do anything more than just sit and whine."

"And Janey," said Floyd. "Can't forget her."

"Oh, Janey," said Patty. "She's just such a great help, standing around and waiting for somebody to tell her what to do. She can't think on her own. If somebody don't put the thought in her head, she ain't havin' one at all."

I was shocked to hear Patty speak in such a way about her own daughter.

"Besides," said McCray. "Your plump son would just eat it all hisself."

Floyd cleared his throat. "I'm growing tired of you talking about my son in such a way."

"Do something about it then," said McCray. "Do something about it or shut your damn trap."

"Both of you shut your traps," said Mary. She positioned herself on her knees by the fire. She held out her petite hands so they could warm. "Fighting like children yourselves. Pitiful." She added a couple sticks to the fire. "That should be enough. The fire's been good and steady for a while now." She examined the meat, sniffed. "Look almost done?"

"How the hell should I know?" McCray said. "Never cooked this kind of meat before."

I heard sniffles coming from beside me. I glanced over. Ellie was no longer looking straight ahead. Her head was down, twitching as she wept softly. Seeing her cry made my heart feel heavy. I wanted to put my arm around her or hold her hand. Something to let her know I noticed she was hurting, and that I cared enough to try to make it better.

Instead, I faced forward again and pretended like I didn't hear her. I felt lousy for doing so because I knew she needed me. I hated myself for being so scared.

Mama rubbed her head, causing her curls to bounce. When she took her hand away, long tresses of curls hung by her face. "I can't believe we're doing this."

"Are you hungry?" asked Patty.

"You know I am."

"Then you will eat. If not, then don't eat at all. We will have the rest. Think any of us like this? Are you more wholesome than us because you're feeling guilt?

We all feel guilty, but we're doing it because it's all we have."

"I am not high and mighty," said Mama. "But I am also not cold to what we're really doing and keeping it from the children."

"Kids don't eat till we eat," said McCray. "Plain and simple. Anyone disputes that can take it up with me."

"I'm leaving," said Ellie. "I can't watch . . . "

She started to turn away. This time, I didn't hesitate to put my hand on her. It clamped on her forearm and pulled her back to me. I was surprised I was strong enough to do something like that. Ellie let out a quiet gasp as she was scooted right up to me.

"Don't," I said. "They'll see you."

Ellie looked pained. Her face, scrunched up, was wet under a sheen of tears. Shaking her head, she said, "Why is Daddy talking like that? Saying those things? I bet it was him who decided to keep the food from us."

I shrugged.

"He's so awful," she added.

I didn't want to agree with her aloud, though she was completely right. He was the worst person I'd ever known.

"Just wait a few more minutes," I said. "We'll get out of here when we know for sure they won't see or hear us."

Ellie nodded.

When I looked at Mama again, I expected her to protest what McCray had said. I could tell she wanted to from how she kept her stiff arms pinned to her sides. Her hands were clenched into fists that tapped her thighs. She looked at the others for support. Nobody offered any. Then she lowered her head, staying quiet. Pretty quickly, the conflict began to drain from her. She walked away from McCray and dropped down on a thick branch that must have fallen from a tree.

Even then, as a kid, I knew I had just witnessed the exact moment all hope left my mother.

McCray's lips curled back, baring teeth. His mustache trailed down either side of his mouth, flecked in ice. From his haughty expression, I could tell he knew he'd won the debate and most likely would win any others moving forward.

I felt squirmy inside, like I knew I should do something to help her, stand up for her. But just like with Ellie, I was too scared to even try. I also knew that if I somehow gained the courage to dash out there in my mother's honor, it would only lead to me getting in trouble and riling up McCray even more. The only person to pay for it would be me.

If Daddy were there, he would have knocked Jack McCray on his self-righteous ass and kicked him to make sure he stayed down there for a spell. I was just a crummy little boy thrust into a situation where he pretended to be grown.

So, I sat.

And watched.

Nobody spoke for a while. The only sounds were the crackling of the fire and soft scraping sounds of the sticks grinding together as the meat was turned.

"How about now?" Ellie whispered in my ear. Her voice made me jump.

I looked at her. Smiling, she cupped her hand over

her mouth. I could tell she hadn't meant to startle me like that and found it amusing that she had. A smile began to tug the corners of my own mouth. I shook my head. "It's too quiet."

"I think you just like being out here with me, Billy Coburn."

Though it was freezing, I suddenly felt as if it were the middle of July. Sweat formed all over me. I must have been so red I was glowing because Ellie began to giggle.

Shaking my head, I turned away from her. If she kept it up, she would get us caught. Though she was absolutely right and I enjoyed having her with me, I was beginning to regret bringing her along.

I scanned the area, watching each of them in intervals. Nobody seemed to feel anxious or guilty, other than Mama. She sat off alone, her face buried in her hands. The only one without a husband. Hers had gone for help weeks ago and most likely wasn't coming back.

Which only meant one thing . . .

The thought died in my mind when my eyes landed on the shovel.

Leaning against the tree, the blade was sullied with compacted dirt. That told me it had been used and very recently.

There was something on the cusp of my thoughts that should have been evident. I knew it even then, but my thoughts and hunger couldn't ease enough for me to realize it. Having Ellie this close to me didn't help my mind to focus, either. She had me so riled and shaky that I couldn't concentrate on anything other than her and how upset Mama seemed to be.

Why had they been digging?

My first thought, albeit brief, was that they had been secretly digging our graves, knowing we would start dropping off one by one just like Chenona's baby. Then it clicked in my mind as if somebody had snapped their fingers in my face, clearing out all other thoughts to make room for this lone realization that made me feel sick inside.

"Oh, shit," I said in a loud gasp. I slapped my hand over my mouth. I felt Ellie's hands gripping my coat and pulling me closer. Now it was her turn to shush me.

McCray looked up, eyes searching.

"What's wrong?" asked Mary.

"Shut up. I'm listening." His head swiveled like a ravenous coyote that just caught the scent of a wounded rabbit. His eyes looked straight at me and I felt a cold bubble form in my bowels. My heart pounded so hard I felt it in my throat.

His head paused, eyes lingered at mine through the mesh of limbs and dead leaves. I doubted he could see me but something made me feel as if he were able to see past the interference and gaze straight into my soul. It felt as if he stared at me for hours, though I knew it only could have been a few seconds.

Then he finally turned his head. "Nothing, I guess. It's time to eat."

"Thank the Lord," said Patty, sliding off Floyd's legs.

Smiles appeared on their faces as they made their way over to McCray.

"What's wrong?" Ellie asked in my ear. "You look like you saw a ghost."

I couldn't speak. My throat felt as if icy hands were squeezing it shut. I kept looking at the shovel. Shaking my head, I told myself they hadn't used the shovel for *that*. There could never be such desperation of hunger that would make anyone stoop to that. Not my mother, definitely not her.

Then I noticed that aroma again. It did smell kind of scrumptious, as if it might taste like deer meat.

My stomach grumbled, then it turned nauseous.

"What?" asked Ellie, desperation and volume coming to her voice.

"It's . . . the baby."

Even in the heavy shadows it was easy to recognize the confusion twisting Ellie's face. I remembered that she didn't know about what James and I saw that morning. Ellie, like most the others, had no clue that Chenona's baby was dead. She'd buried the poor thing with her bare hands.

And they'd dug it back up sometime after.

I could see the deed in my mind as if it were being performed before me. McCray and Floyd, digging like a pair of ghouls, working harder to break through the frozen ground, taking turns, then excavating the infant and darting off into the night.

Not my mother, though. She wouldn't dare participate in this lecherous act.

But then I saw her, joining the others as they approached McCray. For a few moments, her face was tight as if she were in pain. Then it began to relax as the corners of her mouth lifted into a smile as big as the others.

McCray stabbed a big knife into the hunk of meat and began to carve.

Mama licked her lips.

They all did.

Then they began to tear at the meat with their hands, the eating utensils clattering when they struck the ground.

"What baby?" Ellie said, shaking me. I realized she'd been asking me this over and over and was now just starting to hear her. "Billy?"

"Chenona's baby," I said. "He's dead."

Ellie shook her head. My answers were only leading her to more puzzlement about the whole situation. She looked out at them, tearing strips of meat off and stuffing them in their mouths.

I wanted to scream. I could feel it rising in my throat, but the acidic bile stopped it and began to choke me.

Damn them. They really were eating that poor, dead boy.

11.

SMASHING MY HANDS against my ears, I only managed to muffle the sodden chomping of their feast, the slurps and moans of pleasure as they sated their bellies. While they did so, my stomach growled and twisted, shooting jabs of hunger pains and disgust all through me.

In my old age now, I've wondered had I been part of their group, if I would have partaken in the feeding. Had I known the meat had once been Chenona's baby, I like to tell myself I wouldn't have. But that's easy to say after several years and a countless supply of hearty meals in me. I haven't felt such desperate hunger since that time and have lived a good enough life that I probably never will.

I'm sure Mama found herself in a similar mental quandary while listening to the sputters and crackles of cooking baby meat. She'd probably been wondering if she could live with herself afterward.

But when I forced myself to open my eyes, I was aghast to see her smiling. Juice dribbled down her chin. She used the back of her hand to wipe it away. Regretful thoughts were phantoms in her mind in that moment. I don't think she rightly cared if she would ever feel remorse.

Ellie shook me to get my attention, but I wouldn't look at her. I couldn't tear my eyes away from the appalling scene playing out before me.

I'm not exactly sure when Chenona wandered up. I blinked and she was just suddenly there as if developing from the wisps of smoke from the fire. She was dressed this time, but her face was smeared in something that masked her features. There was a section in white that began on her brow and flared around her eyes, narrowing as it reached her mouth and down her chin. Everything else was black.

A skull, I realized.

I remembered Janey saying something about seeing Chenona in a similar attire. Where she'd gotten the supplies to do this to herself, I had no idea. She must always have carried them around with her.

I wondered if she had any suspicion about what they were eating.

Then I understood if she were out here, she must already know. She'd probably seen the grave had been disturbed, the body missing. She'd followed the footprints back to here. Smelled the cooking meat. Saw them devouring it.

God, what was going to happen next?

"You wicked people!" Chenona's voice boomed above the gross chewing and crackling fire.

Mama let out a little squeal and jerked. The meat slipped from her fingers. She tried to catch it, but only managed to swat it to the ground faster. I saw the heartache in her eyes as she picked it up and found bits of dirt and snow clinging to the blackened layer.

"Jesus, woman!" McCray shouted. "You likely scared us all right to death!"

Chenona, arms stiff by her sides, marched into the clearing.

I heard Patty whispering to Floyd about the face paint.

"You desecrated my child's grave!" She brandished a knife. The blade was long and shiny and seemed to have appeared from the air. "You . . . wicked, wicked bastards!"

"What grave?" Ellie asked. I could feel her breaths on my ear. It gave me a squirmy feeling inside.

I turned to her. "I told you. Chenona's baby. That's what they're eating."

In the dark, I watched Ellie's face drop several shades until it looked as if she'd coated her own face in Chenona's white paint.

Mary patted the air. "Please, Chenona, put down the knife."

"I will not!"

McCray stood up, thumbing back the hammer on his pistol. "You will do what my wife says."

Mary looked back at him over her shoulder, her teeth bared. "Don't shoot, you idiot. You'll wake up the kids! Want them out here and knowing what we've done?"

Mama stood up, still holding the knob of meat in her hand. "They'll know anyway. They'll know soon as we get back to the camp."

"Everyone will know!" said Chenona, her teeth gray against the dark paint on her face. "Ahote will know. He will kill you all!"

"Ahote's dead, sweetheart," said Floyd as if he were speaking about the weather. "He ain't coming back. We'd be dead in a couple days, most likely. Same as you. You should eat. There's a little left . . . "

Chenona hissed and marched toward him, the blade shaking. Floyd stumbled back, bumping into Patty. They both fell. Patty hit the ground first. Floyd crashed down on her.

Patty squirmed underneath Floyd. "Get off me, you son of a . . . " She pushed at him, then stopped when she spotted Chenona. Patty hugged him to her, squeezing tight.

Chenona stood over them, the blade an inch from Floyd's face. "Then it will be the law that I tell. You will all hang."

"We didn't kill anybody," said McCray, laughing. "Your maternal abilities did that."

Chenona spun toward him, the knife thrusting the air. "You killed us, Jack McCray. You poisoned the horses. We are here because of you."

McCray's lip curled up, showing teeth. "Shut up, redskin."

"Ahote told me. You wanted us to be in a bad spot. You just didn't figure on the other horses getting loose."

My mouth dropped open. McCray poisoned the horses? That didn't make any sense. What would he accomplish by doing that?

I turned to Ellie. "Did you know about that?"

She shook her head. "It's a lie. Daddy would never . . . " But she stopped talking. I could tell she was struggling with knowing anything at all about her father anymore. "I don't know why he would . . . "

"Our money. It was all we had been able to take with us after the horses began to die. Other than some food and blankets, we had nothing but our savings."

Crying, Ellie shook her head. "I don't believe that."

He was going to kill us all, I realized. Take the money himself to Harvest Hill.

The bastard.

From the ground, Floyd turned to look at Jack. "What's she talking about?"

McCray snorted. "She's lying. She's a damn redskin. Only English she knows how to speak is lies."

"Were you planning to murder us?" asked Patty. "Mary, you knew about this?"

"I certainly did not!"

"She did know," said Chenona. "She knew."

"It's all lies!" McCray flung what was left of the baby meat. "I'm going to shoot her. She's a curse to us."

Chenona's face split with her evil grin. "The law will have your ass, Jack McCray. *All* your asses. You ate my baby. Now, you're going to kill me. They will find out, some day. The children will find out, too. They might not understand what you did right away, but they will figure out."

She turned around, putting her back to McCray. She stood there, waiting. After a short time, she started walking. I expected the mean bastard to put a bullet in her, but he only lowered the gun. He didn't look worried, though I knew on the inside he must have been steaming.

Mary reached for Chenona as she passed. "Listen to reason, please. We're *so* hungry."

"So am I." Chenona didn't even so much as glance at Mary. She kept walking, the knife down by her thigh.

She'd gone a few more steps before Mama slammed into her from the side. Chenona cried out as she was knocked sideways. Her shoulder hit the ground, the knife flying from her grasp. Her legs flew upward, the long cloth dropping back to reveal her bare legs.

I felt tears welling in my eyes as I watched Mama step over Chenona. "You're not telling anyone. No one must know what we've done!"

She raised the shovel above her head. I hadn't even seen her fetch it. She held it with both hands by the handle as if it were an ax. If that were the case, then Chenona was the proverbial wood she was about to split in half.

McCray whistled. "Now I know what Abe sees in you. A damn spitfire."

Mama's eyes were wild, almost feral. Her head shook as she prepared to bring down the shovel.

"For the love of God," cried Patty. "What are you doing, Claire?"

"She'll tell everyone. Help will come and she will tell them. She'll hide in the woods until they arrive. Soon as they do, or soon as Abe comes back, she'll tell him too." She looked at Patty, jaw quivering. "I can't let her do that."

Patty stared at Mama a moment. Then she nodded.

Mama looked down at Chenona. The blade of the shovel trembled.

I had half of mind to call out to her. Another part of me wanted to rush out there and pull her away from all the madness.

But the biggest part of me was too scared and betrayed to do anything.

Only watch through eyes brimming with tears.

Mama heaved, prepared to strike down.

Then Chenona began to chant. Mama halted the shovel's plunge and stared.

Chenona pushed herself up, resting on her elbows. She gazed up at Mama, her coal-black hair hanging behind her back and spilled around her like a dark puddle. That evil grin returned to her face as her tongue lashed and flicked between the mantras. She almost didn't sound like a person, but resembled some demonic thing rising from the pits. The sounds emitting from her throat weren't words that I could decipher. Though I couldn't understand anything, it wasn't hard to guess that what she was saying wasn't good for any of us to hear.

"Make her shut up," said McCray.

Nobody moved. They all only stared down at Chenona as she continued producing grunts and throaty melodies. Her head flung back, back arched and body jerking. She moved with a stiff fluidity, like a coiled snake. Her breasts jutted, straining against the threadbare fabric of her clothes.

Mama looked as if she were about to make another attempt with the shovel. Just as she did, Chenona jerked to a sitting position. Mama loosed a squeal and jumped back while Chenona twitched and shook at her feet.

"That's it," said McCray He stepped forward, lowering the gun. The barrel was inches from Chenona's painted face. "Say hello to the other side." He thumbed back the hammer, again.

"Don't shoot her," said Mary, teeth clenched. "Bash her head in."

Ellie gasped beside me. I stole a quick glance of

her. She had her hand flat against her mouth. Her eyes were shimmery with tears.

McCray's mouth curled upward. He nodded, then turned the pistol around in his hand so he held it by the barrel. "Glad to oblige."

"Don't," said Ellie, her voice quiet. She took a deep breath. I could tell she was preparing to shout.

I threw myself onto her. Ellie landed on her side with a groan. She tried to roll over, but I wouldn't let her. I kept my weight on top of her, putting a knee on either side of her and leaning across her upper half. I put my hand over her mouth.

"He'll kill us, too," I said in her ear.

Ellie continued to struggle.

"Listen to me," I said. "You know he will. He'll kill us to keep us quiet."

Ellie slowly stopped resisting. Her body went limp. She let her head drop against the snow. I took my hand away.

"He's so mean . . . " Ellie sniffled. "So mean."

I didn't say anything to that. I crawled backward off her, then peered back through the gap between the branches.

McCray stood before Chenona, the pistol poised above his head. Floyd had moved behind her at some point and gripped her upper arms to hold her in+ place. Patty stood off to the side, watching, her hands on her chest while her fingers rubbed her throat.

Mary stood with Mama, both watching as well.

"If you're going to do it," said Floyd, "then get it over with."

"We're going to get blood all over us," said McCray. "Good luck explaining that to the kids."

Floyd's face paled. Apparently, he hadn't thought about that.

"We'll worry about that later," said Patty. "Just do it. Kill her."

Ellie began to cry again, but softer this time.

Chenona laughed.

McCray looked down at her. "Somebody say somthin' funny?"

Chenona took a deep breath in and let out another guffaw. "You're all doomed."

"Really, sweetheart? You're the one about to die."

Chenona shook her head. "Your hunger will be so severe you'll *pray* for the release death brings, but the infinite sleep will not come. You will crave the flesh of your own born. You will devour them as you did mine, but it will not stave off the hunger. It is what you will crave above all, and when you feast your bellies will never be sated. You will be hungry until it kills you."

McCray watched her, a disgusted look twisting his face.

"God almighty," said Floyd. "Kill her, Jack. She's putting a hex on us!"

Patty squealed. "A hex? Hexes aren't real, are they?" She looked around at the others for support. "They're not real!"

Mary put her hands to her mouth. Mama only watched, the shovel hanging by her side.

McCray shook his head as if something might have been crawling around inside his skull. He lifted the pistol, again. "Shut your evil mouth," he told her. "Shut it, now!"

Chenona let out another laugh that turned into a

shrill cackle. "If I die, you will never be free of your hunger. It will ravish you on the inside. You will demand the flesh of your born to satisfy you. But it won't. Nothing ever will. You will devour them like you did my born. You will eat them. Each one. And nothing will make the pain go away. So, kill me, Jack McCray. Strike me down! Stomp my head in! Do it! You will never be free!"

McCray's mouth squeezed into a firm line. His mustache peered above his jutting chin. I could tell how desperate he was to kill her from the way his hand trembled. But he didn't.

He lowered the gun.

To Floyd he said, "Get something to gag her. We're going to tie her up."

"You think she cursed us, don't you?"

"Just do what I said, Shumaker!"

Floyd released Chenona's arms, jumped to his feet, and searched around. Chenona sat on the ground, cackling as she swayed back and forth. "You will devour your young. You will devour your young . . . " She licked her lips.

I realized I was shaking all over when I went to wipe the sweat from my brow. I stared at my palsied hand. I wanted to run, to take Ellie and go. We couldn't, though. We were stuck here because there was no way we could sneak away right then.

"I can't find anything," said Floyd.

"There's rope at the camp," said Mama. Her voice was lifeless and dull.

"No time," said McCray. "Use your belt, Floyd."

Without argument, Floyd began to undo the clasp at his buckle. McCray kept his gun trained on

Chenona, but the threat he'd displayed moments ago was gone. He wasn't even looking at the Indian woman anymore. He looked all around, as if trying to make sure nobody was watching.

But little did he know, I had been hidden away and saw everything with his very own daughter.

Maybe that was why they didn't notice Chenona get up. Nobody wanted to look at her. They were too afraid to even acknowledge she was still there, though they all knew their plan was to restrain her until they could think of something better.

I was looking, though, and I saw her scurry away and get to her feet. I nearly shouted a warning to them but held my tongue.

Mama was the first to notice her, but even she was too late.

"Grab her!" Mama yelled.

Cusses and shouts resounded, and the small mob rushed at Chenona as she reached a drooping tree limb. She grabbed one of the branches and turned it upward. Icicles dangled from underneath like frosty roots.

Spinning around, she gnashed her teeth at them. They skidded to a halt on the snowy ground. McCray threw out his arms in front of them as they piled around.

Chenona, eyes wild and mouth wide, leaned back her head. She raised the sharp tip of the icicle to the slant of her smooth throat. She pressed it against her skin hard enough to make a dent.

"Don't do it," said McCray. "Don't do this to us."

Mary held out her hands. "Chenona . . . that's suicide. You will burn."

"I will roam the empty land for eternity. But I will do it to make sure you all suffer . . . "

Patty started to charge toward her. "No!"

Chenona hissed something in her native tongue, then rammed.

The icicle punched into her throat with a juicy crunch. The frozen blade snapped in her hand as blood spurted from her open mouth. Though she had known what she was about to do, her eyes were wide with shock as she staggered back.

The broken tip of the icicle protruded from the hollow of her throat like a tap spewing blood.

"Damn it!" McCray cried. He reached out for her, but she shoved his hands away.

Chenona stumbled a few steps back, then sank to her knees. She gave one last look up at them, then smiled. Her teeth were coated in slick red. Then she dropped sideways. Her back whammed the ground. Snow puffed out around her in a small cloud.

She lay still, arms and legs splayed wide.

They began to spread around her, heads down and gaping.

Mama crouched near Chenona's head. "She's dead."

"No, shit," said McCray. "Damn it."

"What did she do to us?" Floyd asked in a winded voice.

"Nothing," said McCray. "It was a spectacle. A show to put fear in us. That's all."

"It sure as hell worked," said Floyd.

"You're full of shit," said Patty. "It's oozing out your ears."

McCray looked at Patty but didn't say anything.

Mama held up the shovel. “We have to bury her.”

“The hell we do,” said McCray. “She can rot for all I—”

Mama’s head snapped toward him. “Nobody can see this! You idiot! We can’t just leave her out in the open. Jonathan and the boys will go hunting in the morning. If they find her . . . ”

“Then it was suicide,” said Jack. “It was, you know. We didn’t do that to her.”

“Claire’s right,” said Mary. She wiped her mouth with the back of her hand as if something foul was on her lips. She did it two more times before saying, “If she’s found, it will be bad for all of us. Maybe not right away, but it will lead to it. Doesn’t matter if she did this to herself or not. The kids will know about her and the baby.”

“Yeah,” said Floyd. “That will work. The baby died, so she killed herself in grief. The story wrote itself. We don’t have to do anything.”

Patty looked at Floyd as if he were the most amazing man she’d ever known.

McCray shook his head. “I’m thinking Chenona just gave us more meat to hold us over till there’s a break in the weather.”

Nobody said anything for a long time.

Then Mama spoke. “We still can’t leave her out in the open like this.”

On that observation, McCray and Floyd began to move her.

That was when I saw our chance to flee. Their backs were turned to us, their attention diverted. We wouldn’t get another chance like this.

“Let’s go,” I said.

Ellie didn't have to be told again. She sprang up on all fours and crawled into the darkness behind us. Scurrying on my hands and knees, I followed her out from under the brush. Soon as we were free, we spun on our heels and darted into the dark woods.

I kept expecting to hear somebody call out after us.

But nobody did.

We ran as hard as we could. More than once, Ellie left me behind. I would find her waiting for me to catch up. When I did, she would start running again.

We didn't stop until we reached the camp.

And when we did, I found Lenora was sitting on the log Mama usually occupied when we gathered around the fire. She was washed in a dim light that reminded me of photographs that didn't develop right. There was no moon, but the snow provided me enough aid to see the frown on her face as she watched us approach.

"Where have you two been?" Her voice was stern with hints of anger showing.

My stomach dropped into my feet, mugging me of the strength to run. I slowed to a trot, then bent over, putting my hands on my knees while I huffed.

"And did you take the sticks for the fire?" she asked. She stared at me through the darkness for a moment, then I saw the anger seep from her stiff posture. "Billy? What's the matter?"

I tried to speak, but I was too winded. I couldn't find the words. I went to take another step before everything began to shift around me. It looked as if the woods were tilting to the side. I realized I was falling right before my head bounced off the cold ground.

Darkness washed over me, and I was grateful.

My last thought before nothingness took hold was that I hoped I was dying.

12.

I AWOKE IN the wagon, covered in several layers of blankets. I felt sticky and hot, yet somehow cold all at once. I didn't feel sick, but I didn't feel rested, either. Faint daylight filtered in through the cloth. I figured I'd only been asleep for a short while. My stomach felt as if it had teeth and they were grinding together in a fit. The pain was awful, but it was nothing I hadn't already felt before.

Sitting up, I saw I wasn't alone.

Lenora, sitting in the corner, had a blanket pulled up to her chin. "You're awake."

I nodded. My head felt like a rock had been jammed inside where my brain should be.

"Drink." She held out a cup.

When I reached for it, I noticed my hand was trembling. It caused me to recall my shaky hands last night. Then everything came back in a quick rush that made me flinch. I saw teeth, gnashing and chomping, tearing away chunks of juicy meat. Little bits of stringy pieces clung to the teeth, dropping off with the juices that dribbled down chins.

Baby meat.

I groaned.

Lenora frowned. "Drink," she said again.

I had to use both hands to take the cup. Though the air was freezing, the cold water felt great going down. It doused my thirst and washed away the scratchy feeling in my throat. It made my stomach cramp when it poured down, but I didn't care. "What time is it?" My voice sounded odd and breathy.

"Little past dawn. Everybody's hunting."

"Ellie too?"

Lenora nodded. "If you're wonderin' if she told me anything, she didn't. She wouldn't talk to me about last night."

I wasn't surprised. Ellie probably wanted to pretend she wasn't there at all, leave me to be the one to tell what we saw.

"Mama's gone," said Lenora.

I shrank inside at the mention of Mama. I remembered last night—how apprehensive she'd been, then how she'd turned cruel and vicious. "Where is she?"

"Don't know. The McCrays and Shumakers are gone, too. I figure they're up to something. They never came in this morning. Do you know where they are?"

She stared at me. I opened my mouth but had no idea how to start telling her about everything. There was so much she needed to know.

She took the empty cup from me, then placed her hand on my forehead. It felt like she wore gloves of ice. "You're not burning up."

"I'm freezing."

"We're all freezing." She looked at me. "Where did you go last night?"

I needed to tell her what I saw.

So, I told.

She never interrupted me, but she also never gave any indication she believed any of what I was saying. She only stared as the report poured out of me. I had hoped once the knowledge had been shared, I would feel somewhat at ease, but sharing it did nothing to lift the burden of knowing it all. I somehow felt even worse, as if I were hearing the story for the first time myself from a voice that sounded almost like my own, yet it had turned a decibel deeper and sounded scratchy.

When I was finished, Lenora stayed quiet for a short spell. Then she huffed, looked me in the eye. "Show me."

Together, we walked through the woods. I half expected that I wouldn't be able to find the spot again. The snow had done a good job concealing our tracks. I hadn't really been paying much attention to where I was walking the night before. When I did try to take in landmarks or specific surroundings, it all just looked the same. So I'd followed the fire and smells. There was none of that now to aid me.

We went a little further, then I spotted some footprints. I knew they were mine because of the size. I saw Ellie's near them. Like mine, they were halfway filled with fresh snow. I felt a pinch of alarm. Had anybody else seen them? I checked around for others and saw plenty spread all around. Looked like more than one person had been trudging back and forth. That had to mean that most likely our parents knew somebody had been out here, other than them.

We reached the clearing. I knew right away that it looked different now and it wasn't just because I was seeing it in daylight. For one, the makeshift spit was gone. The stick bag was no longer on the ground. I didn't see the shovel anywhere. The logs they'd been using to sit on were also nowhere in sight.

But there were tracks. The snow hadn't buried them all just yet, so sets of depressions were here and there. I reckoned they'd come back and cleared out everything, hoping the snow would hide the rest. Another hour, it would have. The evidence was still there.

"This the place?" Lenora asked.

I nodded.

She walked past me. I stood there as she looked around, examining everything. I know she saw the tracks because she would stop and study them for a bit before moving on.

She made her way to the other side, spotted something, and sank to a crouch. She stared at it for several long moments before calling me over there.

I walked on legs that felt shaky and weak to where she was knelt. She pointed at a splash of red on the snow. "Is this where Chenona . . . ?" She stabbed the air with her fist a couple times.

I knew it must have been, but I still turned and looked over to the brush we'd been hiding behind to see if everything lined up. Seeing the hiding spot in daylight was enough to almost make me scream. There were barely any leaves, and the branches weren't as close together as I had thought. Had we been hiding there without the assistance of darkness, there was no way we wouldn't have been spotted.

"Yes," I said.

"Then this is her blood."

Since she seemed to be speaking more to herself

than me, I didn't respond. She began to sniffle. Lowering her head, her shoulders began to shake. She was crying, I knew. Just like I did with Ellie, I acted as if I didn't realize it. And like Ellie, I wanted to somehow comfort my sister, but I felt too uneasy to try. It felt odd, heartbreaking to see someone I looked up to sobbing like that. The only thing worse, I figured, would have been to see Daddy cry like that.

Lenora's head shot up. "You said they took Chenona with them?"

"Well . . . I think . . . " I shrugged. "We ran off before that."

Lenora got to her feet, quietly groaning. Wiping the tears with the back of her hand, she began to search the ground. I was about to ask her what she was up to when she pointed. "There."

I followed the path of her finger and spotted a smear of crusty blood on the snow. It was a few feet away from where we were standing. Lenora took off toward it. I had to rush to keep up with her as she searched out more blood patterns.

We went deeper into the woods, finding more spills of red along the way. The gaps between the trees began to shrink, pressing in on us. The branches scratched at our clothes like boney fingers trying to stop us.

I wasn't sure how long we'd walked before coming upon a felled tree blocking our way. It looked like a massive, ancient oak tree. Its roots were the sizes of trees themselves.

We climbed up on the trunk. Instead of dropping down on the other side, Lenora just sat there. I was glad to take a rest because I was exhausted.

We had only been there a couple minutes when I spotted the jackrabbit. Well, its head anyway. It was poking up from a hole by some trees a few yards out. Lenora hadn't seen it yet.

I tapped her on the leg. She started to say something, but I put my finger to my lips to quiet her.

She mouthed, "What?"

I pointed to the jackrabbit. She saw it right away. Reaching inside her heavy coat, she removed Daddy's Colt. I should have known she'd brought it with her. I hadn't seen it since I gave it back to her the morning before. That felt like days ago.

She raised her arm, slowly. I put my hand on the pistol to halt her. I remembered what Jonathan had said about my shooting. Though I'd never shot Daddy's pistol before, I knew I had a better chance of pegging the rabbit than Lenora. She couldn't shoot a turd floating in a bucket of water.

Lenora understood I wanted to try for the rabbit, so she let me take the pistol. I put it under my heavy coat to cock the hammer back. It made a muffled clicking sound. I raised the pistol with both hands, setting the sights on the jackrabbit.

It looked around, nose flaring. I didn't relish the idea of slaughtering such a cute animal, but my hunger was louder than my guilt.

I pulled the trigger. The gun boomed in my hand, throwing my arm high. The shot resounded around us like a canon blast.

And the rabbit's head popped in a splash of red.

As the retort of the gunshot faded away, I could hear the ringing in my ears. Through the clamor, I heard Lenora laughing. She patted me on the shoulder.

Then another rabbit sprung from the hole.

"There!" said Lenora in a loud whisper.

The rabbit, bouncing around, saw its dead mate and began to scamper around in circles in a wild fury. It didn't seem to know which way to go.

I shot that one, too. The bullet pegged it in the neck, tossing the furry critter into the air. I was better prepared for the kick of the pistol the second time. My arm only rose half the height it had before.

Lenora squealed beside me. She patted me on the back with such vigor I nearly fell off the tree.

"Let's go get 'em!" There was more strength in her voice than I'd heard in weeks. She held up a burlap sack. I hadn't even seen her bring it out with us.

"Where did that come from?"

"I had it in my coat with the gun. I've been carrying this sack around for weeks in hopes we'd have some meat to put in it. And now we do."

We dropped down on the other side and hurried to the rabbits as if something might charge out of the woods and take them before we had the chance to.

I couldn't believe I'd done it. Two shots and we had food. A good bit of food.

Lenora smiled at me. "I'll start skinning them up when we get back. Good job, Billy. Daddy would be proud."

My throat tightened at the mention of Daddy. If only he could have seen my shooting. I could hear his voice in my head, "Look at that, son! You could shoot the wing off a fly!"

The rabbits lay near each other, their leaking blood melting the snow around them. Lenora held out the sack to me. Nodding, I raised my coat and slipped the gun barrel behind my belt. It felt hot through my pants.

I took the sack and held it open while Lenora dropped the bunnies inside. She took it back, then tied it shut. "Let's get back to camp. I'll start working on these."

"What about Mama and the rest?"

"We'll figure that out later. Right now, all I care about is getting this meat cooked."

I took a step toward the felled tree and spotted Chenona.

I let out an involuntary yell.

Lenora's smile dropped away. "Oh, sweet mercy."

Chenona lay on her side, her back against the tree. Her skin, streaked in frost, was no longer its lascivious shade of brown. It had turned the color of blueberries. The broken icicle still jutted from her throat. I half expected to see either bite marks all over her skin, or that slabs of meat had been carved off her. She was intact, as she had been when she'd died.

I guessed that she'd been lifted up on the other side and dropped, remaining there until we saw her. Most likely, they had planned to carve her up later.

"Don't look at her," said Lenora. "We'll go around the tree."

All the hopeful and delighted feelings that I'd felt moments ago were gone, and with them was my appetite. I was still hungry , but I no longer wanted to eat.

We walked at a brisk pace all the way back to camp. I glanced over my shoulder every so often. I didn't know what I would have done had I spotted anybody slinking around amongst the trees, but the lack of knowledge didn't prevent me from continuously doing so.

It felt like we reached the camp much quicker than we had reached the clearing. I was glad to be back, away from where the deed had happened last night. Away from Chenona. A nuance of relief began to flow through me.

Then it was snatched away when I spotted Mama.

She was standing by the wagon, waiting for us.

"There you are," she said through a smile that looked as if it belonged on someone else. "Where did you two run off to?"

13.

LENORA STEPPED PARTWAY in front of me, her shoulder and right arm shielding me. The sack swayed in her hand. Blood was beginning to seep through, soaking the bottom in dark red.

Mama acted as if she didn't see the kills. That artificial smile held the corners of her mouth too far out, making it look as if her teeth and gums might drop out. Her hair was mussed. The tie still held most of it behind her head while the rest hung free and wild. Dark crescents puffed under her eyes.

"Where were you?" Lenora asked. "You never came back last night."

Mama's eyes narrowed as if she were thinking of an answer. She took a step toward us. I nearly jumped back. Though she seemed mostly normal, I couldn't stop picturing her from the night before—knocking Chenona to the ground, almost bashing her brains in with the shovel. I also saw her on the verge of crumbling into tears when she dropped the straggly remains of the baby meat.

"You were gone all night," said Lenora. "*All* night."

Mama blinked. She bit down on her bottom lip, shut her eyes. She nodded. When she opened her eyes again, they were shimmering. "I was with the other parents, dear." Another step. "We . . . " She shook her head as if hoping it would rattle away the words. "We're not feeling very well . . . "

That was when I noticed Mama hadn't come back alone. The curtain on the wagon moved, then parted. Patty Shumaker's head poked out. She looked over at us, eyes widening. Then her head slipped back inside.

"Why are they over there?" I asked Mama.

"Resting," she said. "Out of the cold for a spell." Mama let out a long breath that turned to smoke in the air. "I think we might be getting ill."

Her stomach emitted a low grumble that sounded like rolling rocks. She put her hand on her stomach and tried to smile.

"Are you all right?" Lenora asked.

Mama shook her head. "No. I should probably lie down as well." Mama turned to me.

I strained to keep myself from shaking. So far, Mama had done nothing to warrant the reaction I was having, but there was something different about her. I couldn't place what it was, but she somehow seemed to radiate it. I tried not to let Chenona's threats reverberate through my head.

"Come lay down with Mommy. That'll help me feel better."

Something that might have been a small bear grumbled. When Mama pushed on her belly, I realized it had been her stomach growling again. She shivered. Her mouth trembled slightly.

Lenora shook her head. "He stays right here with me. He has to help cook his kill." She held up the sack, shaking it.

Mama smiled. "My boy got us something?"

I nodded.

"Look at you, growing into a fine young man already."

"He killed it," said Lenora. "I'm cooking it, so he should dress it. It's what Daddy would have us do."

"Daddy's not here," said Mama. "Billy don't need to dress it if he killed it. He should get to rest, too. Jonathan can skin it quicker, anyhow."

Lenora took a step toward Mama, her chin jutting. "Jonathan's not here, either. He's still out hunting."

Mama smiled. "Then it's you that'll do all of it."

"I want to do it, Mama," I said. "I need to learn . . . "

"No."

"He's staying here with me," Lenora said.

I gripped Lenora's arm and squeezed. Though I appreciated her standing up for me and knew why she was doing it, I didn't like hearing her talk to Mama that way. She'd never done it before and doing it how she was made me uncomfortable. I'd seen people talk to each other like this right before they began throwing punches.

"How dare you," said Mama. "I'm your mother. And you listen to *me*, young lady. I know I ask you to look after your brother for me, but right now, I'm telling you I am going to lie down for a spell. My son is coming with me to keep an eye on me. You do not get to be the mother of me and you damn better believe you ain't his ma, either."

I could tell Mama's words stung Lenora. Her eyes blinked and she had to bite down on her lip to stop her chin from trembling. Lenora put on a bogus smile that rivaled Mama's earlier one. She turned, put the sack on the ground, and faced Mama again. "You're going to have to go through me to take him with you."

Mama's mouth dropped open in shock.

I began to feel hot and squirmy watching them argue. I felt as if I was the one being spoken to that way. I had to stop this before it escalated into something worse.

"Lenora," I said.

Both women looked at me.

I gulped. It felt like I was trying to swallow a rag my throat was so dry. "I'll go with Mama."

Mama snorted. "It ain't no debate, son. You always were. We'll just have the others make room for us."

Lenora looked down at me. I could tell she wanted to argue with me about my decision. Because it was *my* decision. Lenora wasn't about to let Mama force me to go lay down with her. But I wasn't going to let her fight Mama over it, either.

Besides, as far as she knew, none of us had any knowledge about what happened last night. If we kept up this quarrel any longer, she might figure it out. We had no reason we could tell Mama that I shouldn't go lie down with her.

Other than the truth. And if she knew that we knew, well, that would turn really bad really quick.

Mama held out her hand to me. I took it. A nasty smile split her face as she eased me toward her. A putrid odor wafted toward me that had to have been coming from her. I said nothing about it, though. I didn't want to risk offending Mama any more than we already had.

"Get started on the meat," said Mama. "When Jonathan returns, have him help you."

Lenora didn't say anything. She only watched as

Mama led me away. I wanted to look back at my sister but knew if I did Mama would have something to say about it.

"What's got your sister's dander up?" Mama asked.

"I'm not sure what you mean."

"You two have been awfully close the past few days. Something you not tellin' me?"

I shook my head. My voice would probably give me away if I tried to speak. She always knew when I was trying to lie.

The wagon loomed ahead. I had the sudden urge to turn and bolt back to Lenora. I didn't want to go in there with Mama and the other parents. Chenona's threats echoed in my mind. If her curse was genuine, then I was about to be alone with all of them. What would I be able to do if they suddenly decided they wanted to take a bite out of me?

Nothing. It would be a kid against five adults.

As we neared the wagon, I began to realize that I was most likely being led to my slaughter. But I couldn't run. My legs acted as if they didn't know how to do anything other than walk at a lethargic pace.

Mama might have been able to read my mind. Her hand gripped my arm. I could feel it shaking. Her whole body was trembling all over as her stomach made gross popping sounds that reminded me of faraway gunshots.

We reached the wagon and any chance I had of backing out was over.

Mama stood behind me, patting my back. "Go on."

My spine felt as if it was being slowly twisted with frozen hands. I wanted to cry, scream for help, and run away all at once but did none of them. Instead, I stepped up onto the wing. I reached out and gripped the curtain with a shaky hand.

Then I froze.

"What are you waiting on?" Mama asked behind me. "Get in there."

"I don't want to."

"What did you say?"

"I . . . " I took a hard swallow. It made a loud clucking sound.

"You had better stop being so disobedient to your mother. You are not too grown for me to tan your hide."

"Yes."

"Yes, what?"

"Yes, ma'am."

"Better."

Taking a deep breath, I pulled the cloth aside.

A stench like wet copper leached out from inside the wagon, curling around my face. Grimacing, I turned my head and gagged. When I faced forward again, all I could see was darkness around a triangle of light entering through the part in the curtain. It took a few seconds for my eyes to adjust. When they did, I saw James was looking up at me. His eyes were big and round under his nose, a giant hole on top of his head.

Gasping, I almost fell off the wing. I grabbed hold of the hammercloth to keep myself from falling. Staring harder at James, I realized he was gazing back at me, his head turned upward and I was seeing his face upside down. What I thought was a hole in his head was actually his mouth.

His wide-open mouth, as if he'd been screaming.

I lifted my gaze higher and saw why he had been screaming.

Patty and Floyd Shumaker were kneeling on either side of him, hands wrist-deep in his mangled gut. I could see patches of his ribcage showing through the tears in his shirt, coated in tacky pulp. When they pulled out their hands, they were clutching entrails and chunks of bloody meat. They raised their gooey treasures to their mouths and bit down. Blood squirted against their faces, adding to the red smears that were already there. Chewing, their eyes rolled and flickered in their heads.

I opened my mouth to scream but all that came out were whispery cries.

"Get in there, dear," said Mama. Her stomach groaned, causing her to let out a soft whimper. "I'm not going to be so patient with you next time."

I couldn't move, couldn't tear my eyes away from the horrid event in front of me. All I could do was stand there and watch while the Shumakers ate their son.

Movement below James's waist caught my attention. McCray's head rose from between James's spread thighs. Something dangled from his mouth as he chewed, the morsel shrinking more and more. When the tip reached his lips, he sucked, and the rest went between his teeth with a slurpy sound.

I tried to call for Lenora but all I managed to produce was a sound like, "Leeeee . . . " and I doubted she'd been able to hear from where she was.

Mary's head shot up from the other side of the wagon's border, streaked in blood. Her snarling mouth let out a hiss that speckled my face with blood. It was what I needed to shatter the door that had closed on my voice.

Jumping back, I let out a scream that tore through the trees around us like a bullet. I began to drop. I fell through open air only briefly before my back struck Mama. Instead of knocking her over, she stayed upright. Her arms wrapped around me and snatched out of my fall. She yanked me close to her, pressed herself taut against my back.

Something plushy and wet slid down to my cheek and through my frosted hair.

She was licking me.

Her tongue slipped into my ear.

"Let him go," I heard Lenora shout. "Get away from him!"

"Help, Lenora! They killed James!"

"Get away from him!" She yelled again.

Mama's breaths sputtered against my cheek. "I can't let him go. He just . . . tastes so good!"

Mama's moans were loud in my ear as her teeth came down. Hot pain blasted through my head. I began to scream and shake. Mama's moans blended with a moist crinkling noise that drowned out all other sounds. I slapped at her, tried to shove her away. Her hold was too strong.

In my jarred vision, I glimpsed Lenora slamming into us. The impact knocked me into Mama. We both hit the ground at the same time. Mama rolled away from me and scrambled to her feet. Looking up at her, I saw a bloody flap dangling from her teeth. She used her forefinger to push it into her mouth. Then she began to chew, eyes rolling upward in delight.

Lenora rammed her again from the side. They went down in a tangle of arms and legs. Lenora tried to get the higher ground to Mama, but her feet kept slipping in the snow. Mama fought back, wriggling and twisting while slapping at Lenora. Her fingers raked down Lenora's cheek, leaving four jagged scratches behind.

Lenora managed to get on top of Mama, straddling her stomach. She grabbed at Mama's swatting hands, missed, and tried again. She caught one of them and pushed down, planting it under her knee. Catching the other one wasn't as hard since she had two free hands against Mama's one. She pinned it under the other knee.

Lenora had her down. She wasn't going anywhere. It didn't stop her from thrashing and bucking while she grunted and growled. Her teeth were slicked in red. More trailed down her cheeks. I wondered if Mama had been hurt when Lenora attacked her. Maybe she'd bitten her tongue since her mouth was bloody.

Then I remembered the pain I'd felt. I reached up and rubbed my face. Other than being wet and sticky, it felt fine. I didn't notice any wounds or cuts. But when I brought back my hand, I saw it was coated in blood.

"What is this?" Jonathan's voice.

I looked up. Jonathan, Janey, and Ellie were standing a few yards away, watching. Jonathan held the rifle to his chest. Watching everything, his upper lip was curled to show teeth. Janey had her hands over her mouth, observing through the wide eyes above her fingers. Ellie was hugging Janey's side, her face pressed into the taller girl's hip.

"Help me," said Lenora. "We have to tie her up!"

"Tie her?" said Jonathan. "Have you gone mad?"

"Do it!" I yelled. "They killed James!"

"What!" said Jonathan, stepping forward.

"It's like I told you!" Ellie cried, her voice muffled against Janey's coat.

Jonathan looked over at Ellie, then turned his gaze back to Lenora. I could tell he knew something was amiss, but he was lacking all the details so it must have really looked like Lenora had suddenly lost her mind.

"I'll explain later," said Lenora. "Get some rope. Now!"

"Don't listen to her!" Mama cried. "Don't! She's hurting me! Help!"

Lenora flung her head toward me, her yellow hair lashing the air. "Look what she did to Billy's ear!"

Jonathan looked at me, grimacing. "God . . . "

"Get the rope!"

"Come on," Jonathan said to his sister, then he started running toward us. "Get over there with Billy."

Instead of listening to him, Janey dragged Ellie with her behind Jonathan. He saw her still following him but didn't bother with telling her again. I saw they were heading toward the wagon and wondered why they would be doing that.

Then I remembered the rope was in there, inside a trunk.

That was where James was. With him was the other parents. Jonathan didn't stand a chance. I had to warn him.

He was almost at the wagon when I yelled for him. He turned to me.

"Get away from there," I yelled. "They're in there!"

"Who?"

"Your—"

Mary McCray leapt out from the wagon as if she'd been fired from a cannon. Mouth wide and snarling, her eyes were big and white. Arms up, her fingers were bent into claws.

I saw all this in an instant before she pounced Jonathan.

Screaming, Jonathan tried to dodge her attack, but he wasn't fast enough.

Ellie managed to unleash a scream that sounded something like, "Mama!" before Mary pounded against Jonathan with such force that he was knocked against Janey, who brought Ellie down with her.

Jonathan's back whammed the ground with Mary coming down on top of him.

Lenora, straddling Mama, screamed at Jonathan to fight back. She almost went to help him but seemed to think better of it. If she got up, she would free Mama and that would make matters worse.

Mary writhed on top of Jonathan while he screamed and bucked beneath her. I didn't see the rifle, so he must have dropped it in his fall.

Ellie pushed herself up to her knees. She gripped the sides of her face and screamed, tugging at her cheeks as if she hoped to rip them right off.

Janey lay on her side, watching while she cried and shrieked, doing nothing to aid her twin brother.

I looked back at Jonathan. He had both hands under Mary's chin, fingers curled around her throat while lifting her up. Her hands swatted and clawed, shearing his face with her nails. After each slap, she left behind red lines on his cheek, chin, and forehead.

I still had the pistol. I felt its familiar weight pressing against my back. Reaching under my coat, I jerked the pistol from behind my belt. It wasn't like with the rabbits where I didn't think twice before firing. This was a woman. Not any woman, but Ellie's mother. Even in her frenzied state, the decision wasn't an easy one to come to.

Still, I lifted the pistol, training the sight on Mary's face.

"Do it!" Jonathan yelled. "Shoot her!"

My stomach felt as if it had risen to my throat and wouldn't stop until it ejected through my mouth. Quaking all over, I silently asked for forgiveness as I pulled back the hammer. I didn't want to shoot her, but I also wasn't going to allow her to harm Jonathan more than she already had.

"No!" Ellie cried. I felt her hands on my arms, pushing. She knocked my aim sideways. My finger squeezed the trigger. The gun bucked in my hand as the blast rocked my eardrums.

The bullet punched into the ground an inch from Janey's face, throwing up snow and dirt. Screaming, she buried her face in the snow and covered the back of her head with her hands.

Then I hit the ground on my side. Ellie bounced off my other side, rolled, and knocked the gun from my hands. It landed in the snow out of reach, quietly sizzling as the barrel cooled. "What are you doing?" I yelled, trying to get up.

Ellie dropped back down on me, slamming me back onto the ground. Snow puffed in my face, getting in my eyes. Everything blurred as if I were looking through a glass of water.

I tried to roll over. Couldn't. Ellie had me pinned down in a similar fashion that Lenora had done to Mama. "She's trying to kill Jonathan!"

"That's my mommy!" Ellie yelled in my ear. Her breath was hot on my skin.

"Get off of me!"

Jonathan's screams for help were hard to decipher through Ellie's huffing and the growls and snarls of Mary. I could hear Lenora's shouts and Mama's shrieks as well. It was an upheaval of chaos coming from all directions.

"Mommy!" Ellie shouted above the tumult of screams. "Let him be! Get off him!"

Straddling Jonathan, Mary began to slog her hips back and forth. She guffawed and squealed, hopping up and down as if Jonathan were a horse beneath her. "I'm *hhhuuunnnggrrryyyyy!*" Her voice was like two stones grating together.

I squirmed and shook, thrashed on the snow. Ellie started to droop to the side but resituated herself and pushed down harder on me. Even with the possibility of Jonathan being seriously hurt, or worse, Ellie had no intentions of letting me up.

I wasn't happy about doing what I did next because I had always felt a special flutter in my heart when Ellie was around. One look at her and my muscles turned to mud. I would barely speak to her unless it was a mumble here and there. Rarely would I make any sort of eye contact with her because I would find myself slipping away inside their rich, doe-like gaze.

But I had to do *something* to get her the hell off me.

I threw my elbow back. It didn't hit Ellie in the desired location of her stomach as I'd hoped, but it did catch her high on the hip.

Ellie let out an *"Ung!"* and fell to the side, her weight going on one knee. Ignoring the stinging pain pulsing in my arm, I pushed myself up. Ellie tumbled the rest of the way off my back as I dragged myself along the snow.

I spotted the barrel of Daddy's pistol sticking out of the snow. I started crawling toward it, then caught a glimpse of Lenora stepping toward Mary. My sister was swaying on her feet and seemed to move with a slight hobble in her gait. She raised Jonathan's rifle, the stock end inches from Mary's head. Then she stepped forward, bending slightly and bringing the rifle down.

The wood clacked against Mary's temple with a nasty *thwack* that knocked her silent. She stayed on Jonathan, a leg on either side of his lap, swaying at the hips. Her milky eyes gazed forward, lifeless and blank. The smile drooped as her lips went slack.

Then Jonathan swung his fist upward, punching her under the chin. The blow lifted the crazed woman into the air and sent her to the ground beside Janey. She didn't move after that.

I spotted Mama where she'd been pinned under Janey. She was pushing herself up to her knees. Lenora must have left her there to go help Jonathan. Mama was almost standing by the time Lenora saw her. She made her way back to Mama, then repeated the process of whacking the rifle's stock against

Mama's head. She dropped to the ground, limp and still. I hoped she wasn't dead. I felt a subtle brush of relief when I saw she was breathing.

I grabbed the pistol and wiped the snow off the barrel, then dried it on my sleeve. I looked over at Ellie. She was still on the ground, staring at her mother.

"The Shumakers and Jack are still in the wagon," I said. "With James. He's dead. They're . . . eating . . . "

Lenora nodded, then started for the wagon.

"Hold it," said Jonathan. "I'm coming with you." He got off the ground and brushed the compacted snow from his clothes.

As they made their way to the wagon, I noticed more condensation trickling down my neck. I touched it with a finger and looked at it. Blood was smeared across the tip. It felt as if it were coming from higher up on my head.

Reaching up, I tapped my ear and winced at the pain that stabbed into my skull. I did so again, lighter. It still hurt but not as bad.

My ear wasn't shaped right.

In fact, it wasn't there at all.

All that remained was a ragged, wet lump.

Mama had eaten my ear.

I don't remember anything else, except that darkness dropped on me as if I had been covered with a blanket.

14.

I SAW TEETH, gnawing and clacking in darkness. Scraps of food clung to them as drool spilled down bloody chins. A mouth that looked a lot like Mama's opened wide, her tongue shivering like a snake about to strike. Then it lurched at me and snapped shut like a trap.

I jerked awake and didn't know where I was. It was dark and smelled like old sweat and sour milk. The walls were cloth and sticks, pressing in close enough to rub against my arms.

Then I realized I was inside one of the shelters that had been erected near the fire. I could hear the flames cracking and hissing outside. The smell of cooking meat wafted in with the cold. My stomach twisted as I recalled Chenona's baby had smelled very similar.

I turned my head. A blurred face filled my vision. Letting out a holler, I started to sit up and felt dizzy. Everything seemed to tilt.

"Take it easy." Ellie's voice. I blinked and the face cleared. Her eyes were wide as she nibbled at her bottom lip. When she noticed I was staring back at her, the worry displayed on her face softened.

This was the second time in as many days that I'd woken up in the wagon with somebody watching me.

Closing my eyes, I took a few deep breaths. "How long was I out for?"

"I'm not sure. Not real long. You woke up while Janey was bandaging your ear but passed right out again. You remember that?"

My ear. I'd forgotten all about it. But Ellie's mentioning of it seemed to alert the pain. It began to throb, which didn't do my lightheadedness any favors.

"We don't have much in the way of bandages, so she used part of a blanket."

I rubbed my finger across the makeshift dressing. It felt damp, rutted where my ear should have been. I traced a strip of cloth across my forehead and around the back where it was tied in a knot.

I whimpered. "My ear's gone."

"Hey," said Ellie, scooting closer to me. "It's not so bad."

"I'm missing an *ear*. I only have one now."

"Like a pirate."

"Pirates are usually missing an eye, or a hand or foot."

"Would you rather be missing one of those?"

"I'd rather have *all* my parts, thank you."

"You're the first one-eared pirate, then. One-eared Billy."

I looked at her. I wanted to be furious with her for making light of the situation. I had lost an ear, and here she was acting as if I'd simply stubbed my toe. As I said, I *wanted* to be mad. But she was smiling, which seemed to light up her face. And that seemed to brighten the heavy gloom inside the shelter.

I felt tingling in my lungs. I began to laugh.

Ellie took my hand and held it. Though it felt like

a glove of snow gripping me, the touch of her warmed me inside. My heart began to pound.

Then I remembered James. I felt like a real shit for complaining about missing my ear. He'd been killed, eaten by his parents.

And Ellie's.

I wondered if she knew about that part. I figured she most likely did. It wouldn't have been hard to put together.

What had happened after I passed out? I wasn't sure. So, I asked Ellie.

The smile on her face dropped away. "Well, it wasn't too hard rounding up my daddy and the Shumakers. Lenora threatened to shoot them if they didn't come out of the wagon."

"So, they did?"

Ellie nodded. "Tied 'em all up. Your ma, too. They're out there by the fire. Jonathan's watching them like they're prisoners or something."

"They are," I said. "They have to be. If you would have seen what they did to James . . . "

"They wouldn't let me. Your sister and Janey? They covered him up. Wouldn't even let Jonathan see. Was afraid he would go mad and start shootin' them all."

"He probably would have."

"It was real bad?"

The image of James looking back up at me, mouth formed into an O while his midsection lay torn open as his guts were tugged out and gorged upon, flashed in my mind. The cold, dank scent of coagulated blood and sinew seemed to fill the tent.

I nodded. "Horrible." My voice sounded thick and

scratchy. Earlier, Lenora had cold water for me to drink. It didn't look as if Ellie had any.

"They can't bury him," said Ellie. "Not yet. The shovel's gone."

"It was there last night when we . . . "

Ellie nodded. "I remember. Your ma had it."

"Did they ask her where it was?"

Another nod. "She's not talkin' much. Just keeps saying how hungry she is. That's what my daddy keeps saying too. And my ma."

"So, they're okay? After Lenora cracked their heads like that, I thought for sure . . . well, I thought they would be hurt."

"They are. They have lumps right here." Ellie patted her forehead above her left eye. "Fat ones."

Lenora must have really pounded them a good one. Thankfully she had because the situation had been escalating into something disastrous by the second. Not much longer and Jonathan would have been killed.

"I guess everyone knows, then, about what we saw?"

Ellie nodded. Her eyes were grim. "That's why James came back here. I started telling them about it when we went out this morning, huntin'. I couldn't keep it quiet anymore. I figured you was tellin' Lenora, so I told them."

"It's all right."

"No, it's not. James got all riled, sayin' that we was wrong and all. I tried tellin' him we weren't wrong and we saw what we saw. Jonathan yelled at him to keep quiet, that way I could finish. James got mad and said he didn't want hear anything else."

"He came back to the camp?"

Ellie gave another nod. "Jonathan told him if he didn't want to listen, then he should go back and wait for us. That's what he did. But I guess he didn't count on them being here, waiting on us all to come back. That's what they was doin', I think. Waitin' on us."

"Mama sure was. She was sittin' out by the fire when we came up. James had already come back before then, though. We didn't even know he was here."

"I'm sorry, Billy," said Ellie.

I looked at her, confused. "Sorry?"

"For knocking you down. I just . . . it was Mama. You were about to shoot her."

"I didn't want to. She was going to kill Jonathan."

Ellie's shoulders slumped. "I didn't want her to be killed. Didn't want Jonathan to be killed, either. I just . . ." She shook her head, unable to offer me anything else.

"I'm sorry for gettin' you with my elbow."

"I deserved it."

"Naw. I probably would've done the same as you if you were pointin' a gun at my Mama."

A hesitant smile formed on Ellie's face. It looked as if my words had taken away some of her guilt about earlier.

The sound of snow crunching came from outside the tent. Somebody was walking up to the flap. I recognized Lenora's boots when they stepped into view.

"He awake yet?" she asked.

"Yeah," I said.

"Come on out, get some water. Food'll be done shortly."

My stomach shook at the mention of food, but my appetite soured. Though I needed to eat, I had no desire. From the uneasy look on Ellie's face, I figured she felt the same way.

"We have to talk," continued Lenora, "about what we're going to do."

Lenora walked away.

Ellie and I looked at each other. She spoke first. "What do you think she means by that?"

I shrugged. "I don't know. Let's get out there."

15

I CRAWLED OUT behind Ellie. From being inside the tent, the cold outside those thin walls stung my face. A light snow was drifting down from a sky the color of ash. I got to my feet and looked over at the fire. Jonathan stood, the rifle slung over his shoulder so the barrel pointed behind his head. His hair, dangling in his eyes, was sprinkled in snow. His parents sat on the other side of the fire, shoulders slouched. Their hands were in front of them. I figured that was because they were tied. The McCrays were seated to their left with Mama on the right, all sitting in a similar manner.

Ellie was right, I realized. Just like prisoners.

Janey sat off to the side, near where Lenora stood by the meat that was fixed to wood and hanging over the flames. Janey stared off at nothing particular, her hands absently stroking her tangled hair. Lenora was the only one who seemed to be doing okay, probably because she could occupy her thoughts with preparing the rabbit.

I didn't want to go over there. I'm sure Ellie didn't either. But we had to.

We started toward the group. I kept my eyes focused on my sister, purposely avoiding even glancing at the wagon. I figured James was still in there. Even if he wasn't, that was where he'd died and the mess that had been made was probably left behind.

Lenora held out a cup. It was the same one I'd drunk from earlier. I took it and drank without needing to be told to. The water froze my throat as it went down, but just like the last time, it tasted great. When the cup was empty, I gave it back to Lenora. She tossed it on the ground near the stones circling the fire.

"The meat'll be done in a few minutes."

Nodding, I looked at Mama. She was staring at the ground. Her hair was wild and unkempt, hanging around her face like a nest of yellow curls. Her wrists were bound together. A strand of rope led from the bondage down to another pair at her ankles.

I scanned the others and saw they had similar bindings. If any of them tried to stand up, the rope would snap taut and yank them to the ground. I figured that was Jonathan's idea. He was astute in that way.

"How's that ear?" asked Jonathan.

His voice made me flinch. "Gone."

Jonathan nodded.

Janey watched me. Her eyes were red and puffy from crying.

The rabbit meat smelled tasty. Though I didn't have much of an appetite, my mouth began to water.

Then I remembered Mama's stomach, the noises it had made right before she'd attacked me.

My ear was in *her* stomach now. It was my coagulated blood around her mouth.

That pretty much ruined what taste for food I was starting to have again.

I turned away so I wouldn't be tempted to look at Mama again and spotted the discarded rabbit innards piled in a sloppy mound of fur pelts.

I wondered if Jack McCray had done this to the baby while Mama and the Shumakers watched. Had he slit him up the middle? Hollowed him out until there was only the meat and bone? Peeled off the skin?

Had he lopped off the poor guy's little head?

I knew he had most likely done all those things because I remembered how the baby had looked pierced on the spit, his arms and legs tied back as if he were a chicken.

The rabbit meat had browned, so Lenora started to flip it.

I saw Chenona's baby, turning golden with smudges of black here and there as the flames licked his skin.

I saw teeth tearing out chunks, juices spurting. I heard the grunts and moans of pleasure as they chewed.

The squishy clacks of their teeth devouring the meat . . .

"Billy?"

I shook my head. Looked at my sister. She was watching me, concern making her brow furrow. Her eyes were such a clear blue they were nearly the same hue as the snow.

"I'm fine," I told her. The graphic memories were gone, and I could see my sister again. "I am."

She gave me a terse nod. "All right."

Jonathan stepped over to the McCrays, peering down at them. His usual bright eyes were dark with hate. "What was your plan, Jack?"

McCray let out a huff of breath through his nose. His head stayed down. I could see his scalp through the thin wisps of hair.

"Answer me, Jack."

"Jonathan," said Lenora. "Now's not the time . . . "

"It's the only time, Lenora." Jonathan looked at her, a strange smile on his face. "It's all the time we have."

Lenora stared at him another moment before turning her attention back to the rabbit.

Jonathan looked back to McCray. "Well, Jack?" He nudged McCray's leg with the toe of his boot. "Why?"

McCray let out a heavy breath. Without looking up, he said, "I was hungry."

Mary began to sniffle, her shoulders jerking.

Jonathan shook his head. "Not that, you imbecile. Why did you kill the horses and strand us out here to die?"

"Son," said Floyd. "Please, we . . . "

Jonathan spun around so fast it made me jump. He raised the rifle to his shoulder and jacked a round into the chamber as he pointed the weapon at his father. "I'll get to you in a minute. You shut up, you hear me?"

Patty began to cry. "Jonathan, that's your father . . . "

"You shut up, too. Don't you dare speak to me again after what you did to James."

"We were hungry," said Patty. "You don't know how . . . "

"I know plenty about hunger," said Jonathan. "Not once was I tempted to eat anybody. To eat . . . a baby like you did."

Patty let her head drop. Her hair hung over, blocking her bloody face.

Jonathan kicked snow at his parents. Most of it smacked Floyd's leg, but some sprinkled across Patty as well which caused her to jerk and start sobbing louder.

I watched Mama to see what she might do. She did nothing. She just sat there, head down and shoulders slouched like a child being scolded.

Jonathan turned away from his parents and focused on McCray again. "This is all your doing. You did this to all of us."

McCray chuckled. "I didn't put a gun to their heads and make them eat the redskin's baby."

Jonathan swung the rifle down, catching McCray on the knee with the stock. McCray let out a grunt and almost fell over. Mary, gasping, looked up at Jonathan as if he'd just exposed himself to her. Her mouth was wide with shock.

McCray moaned a bit, then looked up at Jonathan. "Why don't you untie these ropes and let's see you try that again."

Jonathan's mouth formed a half smile. "With pleasure." He started to lean over.

"Don't you dare," said Lenora.

Jonathan paused, turned his head to Lenora. "What did you say?"

Lenora didn't waver. "Don't be an idiot. He wants you to untie him."

Jonathan stared at Lenora a moment, then looked at McCray. He seemed to believe her.

"Food's ready," said Lenora. She stabbed the carving blade into the meat's side and began to saw. She looked up at me. "Here, Billy. You shot it, so you get first dibs."

Nodding, I stepped over to her and held out my hand. She put a big chunk on my palm. It was hot, but my hands were so cold that it barely affected me. After I had my piece, Lenora cut one for Ellie, then herself. She let Janey do one for Jonathan and herself.

Once we all had food to eat, Jonathan said a blessing.

Then we ate in silence, none of us taking our eyes away from our parents.

I made myself eat, as I'm sure everybody else did as well. The meat was tender and juicy, but when it dropped into my empty stomach, it sat in there like a rock. Plus, the chewing aggravated my mangled ear.

When the piece I had was nearly all gone, Mama began to moan. Her stomach emitted a sharp bubbly sound that turned into a rattle. I could tell it was painful from the way she squirmed and huffed. "Help me," said Mama, wincing. "I need . . . to eat . . . it hurts . . . "

Patty let out a long wail that made me shiver in my bones. All our heads turned toward her. Even Jonathan's expression showed a hint of concern. "Please," she said.

Mama continued to take labored breaths between her words. "I'm so sorry for what I did. I just . . . want this hunger to stop. It hurts . . . "

Lenora stood up. Not taking her eyes off Mama, she walked over to the cooked rabbit. She used the knife to saw off a chunk, then stabbed the blade back into the rabbit.

She walked over to Mama. "Here," she said, holding out the meat. "Open your mouth."

Trembling, Mama's chin lowered. She titled back her head, keeping her eyes closed.

"Don't you dare bite me," said Lenora.

She placed the meat against Mama's teeth, then let it drop into the dark chasm of Mama's mouth. She stepped back, pulling her hand close as if afraid Mama might try to take a bite.

Mama's chewing was hasty at first, but it was not long before it slowed. Her face began to crumple, as if she'd bit into something sour. She suddenly leaned forward, causing Lenora to jump back with a quick yelp.

Mama's body heaved. A black liquid shot from her mouth, spattering against the ground. Steam rose from the gloppy puddle, melting the snow.

Seeing this made my stomach flip. I felt the scarce contents inside start to rise into my throat. I quickly swallowed it back down and strained to hold it there.

Lenora approached Mama, holding out her arms as if she wanted to help but was afraid to touch her. "Mama! What's wrong?"

Mama jerked and shuddered. She made an awful retching sound but produced no vomit this time. She began to cough. "I can't eat that!"

Lenora began to cry. I could hear her muttering something under the sobs. Though I'm not completely positive, I'm pretty sure she said, "What am I going to do?" over and over.

This time, I didn't hesitate. I tossed the little bit of rabbit meat aside. I rushed over to Lenora and wrapped my arms around her. At first, she didn't hug me back. Just continued to bawl and utter words that were hard to understand. Then it was as if she finally snapped out of it and realized I was there. Her arms squeezed me, and she pulled close.

Mama gazed up at us, moaning. Her stomach produced sounds that a wild animal might make. Hers was not alone, either. Pretty soon, it was a din of growls and hisses.

Jonathan got to his feet. "I can't take this. There's no helping them!"

"Calm down," said Lenora. "Something has to be done."

"The only one that can help is dead." Jonathan let out a humorless laugh. "It was her last trick before going away, her retribution. What can we do to stop this? Huh? You have any bright ideas?"

I felt Lenora's chin rub my hair as she shook her head.

"Didn't think so," said Jonathan. "We have to put them down. Now."

"No!" cried Ellie.

"Jonathan," said Janey. "They're our parents."

"Our parents ate our brother," said Jonathan. "They *ate* him. He was alive while they did it. He died knowing our parents were feeding on him like ravenous beasts. Our parents wouldn't do that. They're . . . something else."

Janey was also crying now. "They can't help themselves. It's Chenona . . . "

"It's their fault," said Jonathan. "They sealed their own fate. I'm going to put an end to this before they get any of us. We keep them alive, they'll kill us all."

"Jonathan," said Lenora.

I tried to turn my head, but Lenora held it in place. All I could see was Ellie, still sitting on the log next to where I had been. Her eyes were aimed to my left, where Jonathan's voice had been coming from.

There was a bout of silence before Jonathan said, "You know I'm right about this. I don't relish the idea any more than you do. Than any of you do."

Nobody said anything else.

I heard Jonathan's footsteps in the snow. Then I heard McCray grunt.

"I'm going to do you first because you caused all this. You'll be in Hell soon."

McCray laughed. "We're already there, kid. We've been there the whole time."

Ellie shook her head, silently pleading with Jonathan. Though her mouth formed the words, they made no sounds.

I listened for the sound of Jonathan cocking the rifle. Then I remembered he already had when he'd almost shot McCray the first time. I figured that instance was more of his temper getting the best of him. That was not the case this round. Jonathan was really going to do it.

"Son," said Floyd. "I'm so sorry."

"Don't speak to me," said Jonathan.

"Do it, son. You have to. We won't be able to stop."

"Dad?" said Jonathan, the anger in his voice starting to slip.

"You have to do it. Put us out of our misery. I don't know how much longer we'll be able to resist. It's like there's something inside me . . . "

"Yes," said Mama. "Something . . . hungry."

Patty sniffled, then said, "So hungry."

McCray snorted, but did not add anything to the conversation.

"Don't say good-bye to us," said Mama. "Just . . . have the others turn away."

"Mama," I said. My mouth was pressed against Lenora's coat, stifling my voice. Tears were starting to fill my eyes.

Lenora began to turn me. I tried to resist her, tried to fight back. My arms would not cooperate. They only held onto Lenora's back, gripping the fabric of her coat while I bawled against her midsection.

Janey's sobs were louder now. I thought I could also hear Patty as well. It was hard to tell, really, because it seemed like everybody was crying.

"Turn around," said Jonathan.

I could still see Ellie and Janey from where I was standing. I supposed he was talking to them since they started shaking their heads.

"Do it," said Jonathan, "or I'll *make* you."

"There has to be another way," said Janey from over Ellie's head.

"There's not. I wish there was."

"Janey," said Floyd. "Do what your brother says. He's right. Look away."

"Don't turn back until I tell you to," Jonathan added.

Crying, Janey pulled Ellie around and put her back to everyone else. Her whole body shook with her sobs.

"I'll make it quick," said Jonathan.

"Do what you have to do," said Floyd. "We love you. Please, forgive us..."

I expected Jonathan to respond, but instead there

was a loud blast that seemed to rattle my head. I felt Lenora jerk against me. Keeping my eyes on Ellie, I saw her shocked face drop to something that looked like confused panic. She looked around, head whipping from side to side as Janey pulled her closer to her.

Then I felt Lenora tugging me sideways.

"Get down," she said through the ringing in my ears.

We hit the ground as another shot rang out. I heard the bullet whistle through the camp, cracking through the branches of the trees on the other side.

Lenora scrambled to throw herself over me while I tried to roll onto my stomach so I could see. We finally settled down with me on my front and Lenora resting across my lower back. Her head was right next to mine.

I expected to see McCray laying on his side, dead, a huge hole in his head. Instead, McCray still sat there, his shoulders hiked up to his ears. Jonathan was on his side near the fire, the rifle pulled up to him and ready to fire. His head turned this way and that as he searched for something.

Ellie and Janey had taken shelter behind one of the tents. I could see them over there, hugging, both heads looking all over.

Not sure at first, it didn't take me long to realize somebody had fired two shots into the camp.

"Somebody shot at us?" I said.

Lenora nodded. "Yes. Almost took off Jonathan's head. If he hadn't turned to the right . . . "

"Who is it?"

Before Lenora could answer, I heard somebody

whistle. It reminded of the harsh whistles Daddy would do to get the horses' attention.

"We gots you surrounded!" Though it was blocked by the trees, the voice sounded close. "That purdy boy better drop his rifle or pigtails gets it. There's a scope on 'er right now. She dead if you don't do it."

Janey.

I looked over and saw Ellie and Janey were still behind the tent. They looked around, trying to find who could possibly have them pinned.

We all tried to identify somebody, but the trees prevented us from seeing much at all.

"I'm a nice feller," said the voice, "but I ain't got a lick of patience. So drop it now. I won't warn you again. She gonna die if you don't listen."

Jonathan looked as if he wanted to stand up and start blasting in all directions. Instead, he let out a moan, then said, "I'm putting it down."

"Toss it away," said the voice. "Off to the side."

Jonathan obliged. The rifle landed several feet away.

"Good boy," said the voice. "We're coming in. No tricks, you hear?"

Jonathan nodded. "No tricks."

"Do you think it's the law?" I asked Lenora.

She shook her head. "Doubt it."

"Maybe they saw how we have them tied up and Jonathan about to . . . "

Lenora looked at me as if she knew a horrible truth that I hadn't been let on to yet. "The law wouldn't have threatened to shoot Janey like that."

I thought about it and realized she was right. Whoever was out there wasn't any kind of law enforcement at all. They weren't here to help us, either.

Most likely, they were bad news.

16.

I SPOTTED DARK shapes slinking around the shadowy spaces between the trees. I was able to make out three men, moving slowly, walking abreast of each other.

Lenora leaned in close to me. “I still have Daddy’s gun.”

I tried to look back at her. “What?”

“First chance I get . . . ”

“Don’t do it. We don’t know how many there are.”

She was quiet for a moment. Then she said, “I’ll wait for my chance. I won’t tell you when I’m going to take it. You’ll know.”

I figured the way I would know was from either Lenora shooting one of them or getting shot herself.

“Don’t,” I said. “There’re a lot more of them than you.”

Lenora huffed. I could tell she didn’t like my reasoning, but I could also tell she somewhat agreed with it.

“Whew-we!” a voice cried. “What have we here?”

The men were only a few steps away from the camp. I could see them through the faint mist that clung to the trees. All wore Confederate uniforms that looked threadbare and ragged, as if they’d been stripped from men killed during war.

The two on either side were tall and lanky, with arms that seemed too long for their bodies. The one on the right had a long, black beard that reached his chest. It fluttered in the breeze like tangle weed stuck on a tree.

The soldier on the left had no hair on his face at all. His eyes were tiny bulbs under an overhanging brow. Thin long hair dangled from beneath his cap.

The one in the middle was the shortest of the three but also the stockiest. His head was wrapped in cloth that had probably once been white but was now a dull grey. Strips dangled like flimsy braids of hair. I saw only one eye peering between the strips as he pivoted his pistol this way and that. I realized the cloth was a dressing that covered most of his face. What glimpses of skin that showed where the bandage sagged was pink and scarred.

The bearded one said, "Want me to fetch the rifle, Lassiter?"

Lassiter, the bandaged one, said, "Go right ahead, Ken." He pointed at Lenora. "Check on her, Wally. I see she's hidin' somethin'."

While Ken walked over to where Jonathan had discarded the rifle, the odd-looking one hurried over to Lenora. He stopped in front of her, arching his back so his crotch was inches from her face. "Got somethin' fer me, darlin'?"

Lenora stared up at him. "I ain't got shit for you, mister."

Lassiter pitched back his head and let out a guffaw that turned to a cough. Wally seemed a tad hurt by Lenora's comment. He looked around as if he did not know what to do.

"*Shee*-it," said Lassiter. "Damn firecracker, that one. I knew she'd be. Didn't I tell you? I tolt you that, didn't I?"

Wally, looking as if he were holding back tears, nodded. "You shore did, Lassiter."

Lassiter whistled. "Saw that photograph and knew she was a firecracker. Don't have looks like her and not be one. You gots to be. Right, love?"

Lenora looked as if she might be sick. I suddenly felt hot and mushy inside. I wondered how they had seen a photograph of Lenora. What were they doing here? How'd they know about us?

Lassiter let out a long, good-humored sigh. "That was fun. Wally, the girl's hidin' a pistol under her coat. See how it's bulgin' out below the two thangs there that should be bulgin'?"

Wally looked down. A goofy grin split his face. "Yessir, I do. I sees it now."

"Grab it? We don't want her gettin' any bright idears."

Wally licked his lips. "Glad to." He started to bend over, reaching out with his left hand.

Lenora snatched Daddy's Colt from under her coat and tried to swing it up at Wally. She wasn't fast enough. Plus, the gun was heavy, which slowed her momentum. She'd barely gotten it partway up before Wally snatched it from her hand.

"Nice one," he said, clucking a laugh. "Had to go fer it, huh?"

Lenora shrugged.

"Slap her," said Lassiter. "Hard enough to learn her. But don't bruise that pretty face, huh?"

Wally nodded as he tucked the Colt behind the

belt of his trousers. He stared at Lenora a moment, then flung out the back of his left hand, whacking her above the ear. Her head jerked sideways, knocking against mine hard enough to cause light to flash in my eyes. In my ringing ears, I could hear shouting. I recognized Jonathan's voice and maybe even Mama's.

Moaning, Lenora let her head drop into the snow.

"That good?" Wally asked.

"Good enough." Lassiter's head slowly swiveled, taking in everything. "I can't even try to guess just what in God's name is goin' on here. Color me intrigued, fer shore. But before we's get into all that, I think everybody needs to be searched to make shore they ain't hidin' no other weapons."

I noticed Jonathan's face. He looked as if somebody had just told him he would have to roll in the snow without his clothes on.

Ken also noticed. Chuckling to himself, he walked over to where Jonathan sat. "Whatcha hidin' there, boy?"

Jonathan huffed through his nose. He looked away. "Pistol."

"A pistol? Ohhhh." Ken kicked Jonathan in the leg. Jonathan didn't fall over, but he let out a low groan to stifle his pain. "Then hand it over. I'll add it yer rifle." He held up Jonathan's gun with pride.

Jonathan reached behind his back. Ken pulled the rifle to his shoulder and trained it on Jonathan's head. "Slower, boy."

Jonathan moved his arm with caution. He reached under his coat and tugged out a pistol. I couldn't see it very well from where I was, but I figured it must have been Floyd's. He'd probably disarmed his father before tying him up. That meant somebody must have McCray's.

Ken took the pistol and dropped it in the pocket of his Confederate coat. Then he moved over to Janey, grinning ear-to-ear. "You got anything I need to grab from you, darlin'?"

Janey grimaced, then shook her head.

"I think I need to check to be sure."

While he checked Janey and Ellie, Wally took his time checking Lenora. Then he moved over to me. He began to search my pockets. I heard something rattle from my pocket. Wally's eyes widened.

"What's this?"

I realized what it was right before he tugged out Daddy's watch.

"No," I said.

"Lookie here," said Wally. Holding it by the chain, he let the watch slowly turn while he examined it. "That cost a pretty penny, fer shore."

"Don't," I said in a quivery voice. "My daddy gave me that."

"Yer daddy gave you that?" he said, mocking me. Then he laughed. "And now yer givin' it to me. I thanks ya, kindly."

I choked back the sobs that wanted to come.

"You're a real bastard," said Lenora. She rubbed her head.

Wally shrugged. "I guess I am."

I looked at Mama, hoping she might say or do something to stop Wally. But it was pointless. Mama hardly even acknowledged him. She was too busy shaking and twitching to notice much else.

"That all?" asked Lassiter.

"Yep," said Wally. "Just the one it looks like. And my new watch." He dropped it in his pocket.

Lassiter faced us. He cleared his throat. "Well, now that that business is out of the way. What say you's explain what in the hell's goin' on here."

Ken walked backward. He had Jonathan's rifle slung over his left shoulder while holding out his pistol with the other. The barrel pointed at Jonathan. "Looks like kids rebellin'."

Lassiter walked toward the McCrays. "That what's goin' on here?"

"Untie us," said McCray. "That one over there was about to shoot us before you showed up." He thrust his chin in Jonathan's direction.

"Son of a bitch," said Lenora.

Lassiter pointed at himself, then to McCray. "Him or me?" His craggy lips stretched to show brown teeth. I supposed it was a smile but wasn't exactly positive.

"Who are you?" asked McCray. "Are you here to help us? To harm us? What?"

"Well," said Lassiter. "That all depends, I reckon."

"Depends?" asked Floyd. He looked at McCray, shook his head as if confused.

"On if you's can help me."

I noticed his eyes were locked on Lenora. She tried to hold his gaze, to show him she wasn't afraid. It didn't last. She turned away, which caused the bandaged goon to snicker.

Lassiter slipped his pistol into the holster on his hip, letting his shabby coat fall shut. He reached into a pocket and removed something flimsy.

A photograph.

He turned it so we could all see it. I recognized it right away, as did Lenora. We both gasped when we saw ourselves with our parents in the picture.

Even Mama was looking. Shivering, her eyes narrowed. "Where did you get that?"

Lassiter laughed. "Look fa-meeler?"

"My husband took that with him when he hiked out of here for help."

I didn't know that, and from the way Lenora was reacting, she hadn't known either. He must have taken it from the trunk in the wagon at some point.

Lassiter tapped the picture where Mama's face was. "Been staring at that face a whole bunch. But not as much as this 'un." He tapped the captured image of Lenora hard enough to make the photograph bend back. "Been *dreamin'* 'bout 'er. Dreams like that keep a man warm on these cold, snowy nights."

"Where's my husband?" asked Mama. "Is he all right?"

Ignoring the question, Lassiter turned and looked at McCray again. "Why that boy 'bout to kill y'all? Why y'all tied up?"

"They want to eat us," said McCray.

"Liar!" Jonathan started to get up, but Ken was on him in a flash. He swung his arm down, clocking Jonathan on the forehead with the barrel of his own rifle. Grunting, Jonathan fell back, landing on his side. Blood trickled down from the wound, clinging to his eyebrow and spilling over his temple. Jonathan put his hand against it, moaning.

"Leave him alone!" Janey cried.

Lassiter began to laugh again.

I noticed Patty staring at her son, shivering as her

eyes locked on the trickle of blood. She turned to Floyd, whispering. He nodded. They said nothing to Jonathan. Didn't even ask if he was all right.

Mary had also noticed the blood. A string of drool dangled from the corner of her mouth.

Lassiter whistled. "Eat ya? These kids tryin' to eat y'all?"

McCray nodded.

"I smell something," said Lassiter. "Weird thing is, I heard y'alls horses were dead and disappeared. Why's that mean I'm smellin' horseshit?"

McCray's lips mashed into a tight line.

Mama gasped. "You've seen Abe. Tell me where he is. What did you do to him?"

As if Mama hadn't spoke at all, Lassiter leaned in closer. "Y'all also covered in blood. Got it all over yer faces. I feel like yer not tellin' me the truth."

McCray's lip curled.

Lassiter sighed. "Have it your way." He looked at Lenora again. The skin at the corners of his stiff mouth twitched. "Wally?"

The goofy man looked at Lassiter, his mouth hanging open.

Lassiter sighed. "Grab 'er fer me and head to the wagon. I'll be right behind you."

"No!" Mama cried.

Lenora, shaking her head, started to crawl away. Wally walked over, smirking as he started to lean down.

Lassiter turned to Ken. "Throw some more logs on the fire. It's damn-near dead. Getting' cold out here."

I could hear Janey and Ellie gasping and crying as Wally approached my sister. Whimpering, Lenora swatted at Wally's hands. She slapped one, which only made him laugh. He hopped, giggling like a child each time he reached for her and got himself smacked.

A game, I realized. He was playing a damn game.

I wanted to do something to protect her as she had protected me all my life. I didn't have any idea how to go about it. I looked around for anything close that I could grab and use for a weapon. There was nothing. So, I hobbled over to Lenora on my knees. Wally turned just as I reached her, the grin on his face big and goofy.

He saw my fist coming and the smile drooped.

Then my hand connected with his chin. Pain jolted through my arm, locking it up. I hollered, then fell back, landing on Lenora's legs. When I looked up, I saw Wally was still crouching but now shuffled back as he tried to keep his balance. Then he dropped onto his ass, his throat clucking when he landed.

There was a buzzing in my head that caused my hurt ear to throb. It also seemed to drown out most of the sound around me. As it started to fade, I began to hear Lassiter laughing. The sounds of Lenora's voice tried to cut through, but I couldn't make out what she had to say at first.

Then it cleared enough that I understood.

"Look out!"

I turned in time to catch Wally looming over me. Gone was the goofy expression and idiotic look about him. His lips were peeled back, baring his rotted teeth. I noticed a scar on the tip of his nose right before he reached down and grabbed me.

He lifted me off the ground as if I were a kitten. In my twirling vision, I glimpsed Lenora reaching for me, Mama crying for me, and Ellie and Janey bawling. Then all I saw were trees, whipping around as if on a top that had been just let loose. I felt nothing under me which made me think Wally had tossed me into the air.

My idea was confirmed when my back pounded the rig Lenora had constructed for the rabbit. I came down on it, the stick legs snapping as my body mashed the rabbit to the ground. I looked over beside me and saw if I had gone another inch I would have landed in the fire. It was popping and lashing since Ken had stoked it and added more branches.

I didn't feel the pain right away. I had gone into some type of numbed shock when I realized how far my flight had been. Wally didn't look like the kind of person to possess the kind of strength he displayed, which meant my punch knocking him down wasn't because of my amazing fighting abilities. I had simply caught him off guard.

And embarrassed him.

I spotted him marching toward me, that blank look showing even more viciousness. I knew this attack would be worse than the one before it.

"Hold it," said Lassiter. "The kid's down. You proved yer point."

"I'm not done," said Wally.

"You are," said Lassiter. "Until I say yer not done."

Though Wally stopped walking, I could tell he didn't want to.

"Take the girl to the wagon," Lassiter repeated. "She—or anybody else—gives you any trouble, I'll have Ken shoot the boy."

Ken snickered, then gave me a look that showed

he hoped somebody gave Wally some trouble. My back felt as if it were being scraped by icy claws.

Wally let out a few clucks before turning around and grabbing Lenora's wrists. In one quick jerk, he had Lenora up on her feet. Gasping, Lenora stared at him, her eyes blinking rapidly. She looked as if she were about to say something, but Wally spun her around and gave her a shove.

"Move," he said.

"Leave her alone," said Mama. "Not her . . . "

Lassiter walked past Mama, gave her a nod. "Only be a few with yer daughter, ma'am." The loose strips of his dressing flopped like inverted bunny ears. "Just sit tight."

Mama's stomach groaned which elicited a groan of her own. She lowered her head and winced. Lassiter paused a moment, peering down at her. He glanced at Ken, who was grimacing. Neither of them spoke about it and Lassiter moved on.

Once he'd gone a few feet away, McCray and Floyd leaned closer to each other, looking past their wives. I could tell they were talking from the way their heads moved. Ken also noticed and kicked snow at them. "Shut up," he said. "Don't get any idears, if you know what's best fer ya."

McCray looked up at Ken. "Who are you people? Soldiers?"

"Once a solider, always a soldier," said Ken.

"The war's over, boys," said McCray.

"It's never over," said Ken. "And shut up or I'll put a bullet in that purdy wife of yers."

Mary gasped.

McCray laughed. "She wants to die. You'd be doing her a favor."

Mary's head whipped toward McCray. "You're such a son of a . . . " She shook her head, unable to speak.

Ken looked around. "One of these kids yers?"

McCray didn't say anything.

Ken's eyes landed on Janey and Ellie. He looked back, grinning. "That's her over yonder. The redhead. I likes 'em with hair like that."

Ellie squirmed closer to Janey, who put her arm around her.

"Yeah," said Ken. "That's her, fer shore. Looks a lot like yer wife. Same eyes. And nose. She looks like she might taste sweet. Maybe I'll see if Lassiter'll let me and her have a turn in the wagon when he's done with the other girl."

McCray held his silence. Not that I expected him to be an honorable father, but I couldn't believe he wouldn't stand up for his daughter at least a little bit.

Ken laughed. "That's what I thought. So sit there and shut up, or it's *you* I'll put a bullet into since nobody else matter to you."

McCray looked down at the ground and said nothing else. Nobody else decided to speak up, either.

My back was starting to really hurt from lying on the rabbit, so I rolled over. That helped some of the pain there, but I still ached all over from my rough landing. I was about to attempt sitting up when I spotted the knife.

I had to bite down on my lip to stop myself from crying out with glee. The knife was on the ground beside the meat. I remembered it had been embedded in the rabbit's side after Jonathan had finished carving off some pieces for Janey, Ellie, and himself.

I must have knocked it out when I landed on it. Thankfully, I hadn't been stabbed. But even better than that was nobody had noticed the knife was there at all.

Checking over my shoulder, I saw Ken wasn't looking at me. He was watching Wally and Lenora at the wagon. Lassiter had almost reached them. Wally was saying something to Lenora. She shook her head, started to speak, but Wally grabbed her arm and shook her. Her words turned to shrieks.

As angry as it made me to see my sister being abused in such a way, I knew there was nothing I could do about it.

Not yet.

My eyes returned to the knife. It was mere inches from my fingertips.

Ken started to laugh. Another glance at him, and I saw he still hadn't looked in my direction. I reached out, put my hand on the hilt, and slid the knife toward me. Then I picked it up and stuck it under my coat. Putting it behind my back, I slid the blade behind my belt just as I had done with Daddy's pistol.

Knowing I had the knife, my heart began to pound. I checked on Ken again. He still hadn't even looked at me.

An idea to try using the knife on him tiptoed through my mind. It was faint at first, but the longer I stared at him, the more I wanted to do it. If I could get over there, get him in the leg, then Jonathan could get back his rifle.

But that left Lenora with the other two. I doubted they would be willing to trade Lenora for Ken. The soldiers didn't seem too loyal to each other in that way. I would have to wait for another chance.

Lenora's original plan, I realized, but now it was up to me. I would much rather have Daddy's pistol like she'd had, but the knife was better than nothing.

I looked over at the wagon. Lenora was still refusing to go inside. I was glad that she wasn't allowing them to control her, but I also didn't want her resisting so much it caused them to harm her even more.

Then it dawned on me why she didn't want to go into the wagon.

James was still in there.

Wally, evidently tired of Lenora's refusals, climbed up onto the back of the wagon. He started to climb inside. He paused. His body went rigid. Then he let out a loud squeal of alarm as he launched backwards. He landed on the snow at Lassiter's feet.

Lassiter kicked him in the back. "What the hell's the matter with you?"

"There's a dead kid in there!" Wally shouted in a winded voice.

"The hell you just say?"

Wally shook his finger at the wagon. "Look fer yerself!"

Lassiter poked his head in. He stayed that way for several seconds. Then he turned around to face us all again.

He started back toward us. Even through the bandages, I could tell he was a combination of angry and confused.

17.

WALLY SHOVED LENORA to the ground beside me. Gasping, Lenora sat up and pulled me close to her. Her arms squeezed me too hard, making it almost impossible for me to turn and watch Lassiter as he paced a gully into the snow.

He pointed at the wagon. “Whose kid is that?”

Nobody spoke. I didn’t understand why nobody wanted to tell him. Maybe they feared admitting what had happened, a part of them that still thought they would get in trouble for what they did. Even as a kid, I knew Lassiter and his boys were only here to cause more trouble. How they knew about us and why they decided to come here was a mystery.

Lassiter reached into his coat, brandishing his pistol. “I’m sick of this shit. I knows I was havin’ some fun with you before, so you might not take me serious now. But if somebody don’t start talkin’, I’m gonna start shootin’.”

He looked around, spotted Janey and walked over to her. She saw him coming and began to make sounds like a wounded puppy. She shook her head hard enough to make her pigtails flop. He lowered the pistol to her face, holding it so the barrel was only an inch or two from her cheekbone. The way she was sitting, if she were to get shot, the bullet would surely pass through and get Ellie as well.

Jonathan saw this and hollered. He started to move, making on all fours before Ken kicked him in the gut with such force, Jonathan flipped over and landed on his back. The air burst out of his lungs. He made barking sounds as he tried to breathe.

"Good one," said Lassiter. "How's he s'posed to talk if the bastard can't even catch his breath?"

Ken's cheeks reddened. He shrugged. "I dunno."

Lassiter let out a breath that stirred the limp bandages. "I should confess somethin' 'bout me. I'm not what they call a patient man. My daddy always tolt me my lack of waiting on things to unfold as they oughta would get me in trouble." He shrugged, rubbed his bandaged face. "He shore was right 'bout that. We's all were hunkered down in the ditch when a small party of Federals came up on us. Our orders were not to attack, but to report back what we saw. Well . . . my damn impatience, you know. I knew by the time I got back to camp, the damn Northerns would be gone. So, I hauled ass out of there, ready to wipe 'em out. I planned to put their heads on spikes when we were done so their buddies could see 'em and know what they's up against."

Wally and Ken laughed at that, though I don't think Lassiter was trying to be funny.

"I ran right out there ready to shoot, but one of them was quicker. I admit it. He got off a shot just as I was about to shoot. His damn lead ball went right up my barrel as I went to fire, and my damn gun blew up in my face."

"Damn shame," said Ken.

Wally nodded. "Lassiter was always good with the ladies. Had a face that made 'em shiver in their drawers."

"Watch it," said Lassiter. "Ladies and children present."

"Sorry," said Wally, lowering his head.

"Anyhoo," said Lassiter, "what I'm tellin' you is that when I ask you again what the hell's going on here, you's gonna tell me or I'm 'bout to shoot this girl in the face."

He raised his pistol, leveling the barrel on Janey's face. She stared at it, sniffling, her mouth tight around her teeth. She hissed through her nose. Lassiter pulled back the hammer. It sounded like a thick branch snapping as it resounded off the trees around us. Janey flinched, her whimpers pushing against her lips. She kept her mouth shut, holding them in.

"Stop," said Lenora. "Leave her alone."

"Gots to show you all how serious I can be."

"Please," said Lenora. "Don't hurt her . . . " She began to bawl, her words turning to blubbering nonsense.

"I'm not going to hurt her," said Lassiter. "I'm going to kill her." He sighed. "Sorry, little lady." His finger started to squeeze.

I leaned forward and blurted, "James!"

Lassiter jerked. For a moment, I feared my sudden shout had startled him enough to finish squeezing the trigger. Thankfully, he was quick to pull his finger away. He looked over at me. "What'd you say, boy?"

I tried to answer him, but I couldn't find my voice. All that came out were stuttering squeaks. I could tell that Lassiter was not in the mood to wait on me to catch my bearings, so I strained until the words came out. "James. He's . . . theirs."

I pointed at the Shumakers.

Lassiter looked at them, then back to me. "What happened to him?"

"They . . . " My chin trembled. I gritted my teeth to keep them from chattering. I took a deep breath through my nose and let it huff out. "They ate him."

Silence fell over the camp. Lassiter peered at me for several long seconds before he turned to look at the Shumakers. "They ate him, he says." His voice was low, as if he'd been speaking more to himself than anybody else. He pointed at them, then wagged his finger back and forth. "That's why they's tied?"

I nodded. The movement caused my ear to flare up.

"Why they's tied?" His finger hovered at Mama, then made its way toward the McCrays. "They eat him, too?"

"I think the McCrays did. Mary attacked Jonathan."

"Jonathan?"

I slowly nodded my head toward Jonathan. He was no longer laying down. He was sitting, his legs pulled to his chest while he hugged his knees.

"Ah," said Lassiter. "Mary attacked *him.*"

I couldn't tell if he believed me. The tone of his voice gave me no hints.

"And this one?" He pointed at Mama. "She's yer ma?"

"Yes."

"I see. And why is she tied up?"

I gulped. "She ate my ear."

Lassiter gave me another long look. "You ain't shittin' me?"

Turning my head, I pointed at my bandaged ear.

"No," he said. "I guess yer not."

I heard Ken mutter, "Damn."

Wally just stood there, that goofy grin on his face again, as if we were telling jokes he didn't understand.

"Ken," said Lassiter. "Get over here and untie her feet."

"Don't," said Lenora. "You can't do that."

Ken seemed hesitant to move from where he stood near Jonathan. "Um . . . " He lifted his cap, rubbed his curly hair. "I don't know, Lassiter."

Lassiter stared at him through the bandages. "What?"

"I mean, you heard the kid."

"I shore did."

"I don't know if I wants to be messin' with somebody that's been eatin' ears and whatnot."

"You believe that's what happened?"

"Don't you?"

"Hell if I know. But I do wants to know fer shore. So, come over and untie her feet before you go and piss me off. I want to watch her eat somethin'."

Gulping, Ken slapped the cap back on his head. I watched what color he had drain from his face. "Yes, sir."

"That's better."

Ken walked like a chastised child over to where Mama sat. He muttered, "Shit."

She looked up at him. "Please leave us be." Then her stomach loosed one of those sawing groans.

Ken looked at Lassiter. "You hear that?"

Lassiter nodded. "The hell was it?"

"Her stomach."

"She must be hungry. If she's eatin' ears and whatnot." He laughed.

Ken laughed as well, but I could tell it was forced.

Mama's stomach drowned out their laughter, then killed it altogether. Ken took a step back.

"For the love it all," said Lassiter. "Stop bein' a shit and untie her damn feet!"

"I am!" Ken passed the rifle to Lassiter, then sank to a crouch. Mumbling under his breath, he started to reach for the rope between Mama's ankles with arched fingers. Just as he started to work at the knot, Mama's stomach let out another sharp groan. Jumping back, Ken let out a wild shriek. His feet slipped through the snow, rose in the air, and dropped him on his back.

Lassiter and Wally erupted with laughter.

Sitting up, Ken slapped at the ground to steady himself. "You see that, Lassiter? She damn near took a chunk outta me!"

This elicited even more laughter from his comrades.

Wally snorted. "That was 'er stomach, dumb shit!" He slapped his thigh and let out a loud guffaw.

While they were busy laughing, I reached behind my back and curled my fingers around the hilt of the knife. I was a short distance from Lassiter and Ken. If I could get to Lassiter in time, I should be able to plant the blade into his gut. The bandaged leader had his pistol in one hand and the rifle in the other. I doubted he'd be able to get off a shot with his pistol in time, and there was no way he'd be able to get Jonathan's rifle primed to fire with one hand.

But I would have to get there without Wally seeing me as well. I didn't think I would be able to do that before getting a bullet put into me. I shook all over with the want to make a go at it. I had to hold my breath to steady my heartbeat. When I finally peeled my fingers off the hilt, I could feel sweat trickling down under my shirt.

The laughter died. Lassiter stared at Mama. Behind the bandages, I saw him run his tongue across his disfigured lips. "What's wrong with her, boy? Why'd she do that to your ear? She ill?"

I nodded. "Ill."

"What kinda illness makes somebody eat their kids? Where'd she even catch an illness like that?"

To my surprise, I answered him in truth without any hesitation. It just flowed right out of me. I told Lassiter everything, leaving out no detail that I could remember. When I was finished, Lassiter didn't react. He just continued to stare at Mama.

Wally whistled. "This place is jinxed, Lassiter. Maybe we oughtta ride out."

Lassiter shook his head. "Not yet. We came here for a reason. I'm not leaving yet." He looked down at me. "You said the redskin woman did this to them? She put the juju on them because of the baby?"

I nodded.

Lassiter harrumphed. "Well, that there's a story *almost* batshit crazy enough to believe. I wants to know more, though. Wally? Go fetch the redskin, bring him over here."

"Yes, sir." Wally looked almost relieved as he

rushed off through the trees, making his way to the trail.

Lassiter sighed. “Maybe he can explain some things.”

Mama’s stomach didn’t let up. The more she stared at Lassiter, the louder it became, a sawing drone that sounded like a den of angry bears.

I tried to ignore it and focus on what Lassiter had said to Wally about fetching the Indian. I had no answer for any of these questions until Wally returned with our new guest. Walking behind a tall, dark man, Wally shoved him with the butt of his rifle. “Move,” he told the much taller man. They stepped into view, the shade of the snowy trees sliding off them bit by bit.

My breath snagged in my throat when I saw the man with Wally. He looked disheveled and exhausted. The bruises, cuts, and welts were proof he’d been ruthlessly beaten. A lot. His hair was filthy with dirt and ice.

Though his face was swollen and bruised, I still recognized him.

Ahote.

18.

LENORA AND I shared a look. Her pale face was twisted with confused fear. I figured her mind was a rush of thoughts same as mine.

Ahote made his way further in. Mama's stomach seemed to roar, which caused Ahote to turn her way. He saw her, gasped, and spoke something in his native tongue. Then he looked at me and his already wounded face turned grim.

"Where's Daddy?" Lenora asked him. "Is he with you?"

Ahote didn't look up.

"Shut yer trap, girlie," said Lassiter. To Ahote, he said, "On your knees right here." He stomped the ground in front of him with the heel of his boot.

Ahote obeyed his command without any protest. Lassiter slapped his hand down on Ahote's shoulder. He ran his tongue across his dry, scarred lips. "You know this here redskin?"

Lenora nodded. "He left with our father."

I felt antsy, squirmy. Like there was a hot stream rushing under my skin. "Where's he?"

Lassiter hocked up something wet from his throat, turned sideways, and spat it on the ground. It smacked the snow with a squishy plop. "He tells me he was yer guide."

I nodded.

Lassiter smiled. The teeth that showed between the scarred lips were brown. "Since you shared a story, I thinks I'll share one with y'all. I see how it's only fair. See, we been set up down at Devil's Pass for a spell, trying to outlast the weather. One day, these horses just come trottin' right up. I could tell they hadn't eaten in a few days. We's thought we some lucky sons of bitches to just have some horses find us like that."

"Horses?" said Lenora.

Lassiter laughed. He looked at Wally and Ken and they joined in. Ken's eyes kept glancing down to Mama, like a man standing next to a coiled rattler.

Lassiter nodded. "Pay attention, girlie. You's look like you's had some ed-ur-cation, but you's actin' dumb as hell."

Lenora gasped as if the comment had offended her.

I watched Ahote. He still stared downward. My eyes moved to the left, just enough to see over his broad shoulder. I saw Mama. Her mouth was moving, teeth grinding like stones. Her eyes were feral, glancing all over as if she didn't know where to look.

"Later that day, this redskin wanders up with yer daddy. They follered the horses' tracks right to us. One look at us and they acts like they just stumbled across God. The white man tells us all 'bout the bad luck—the horses and all. Tolt us 'bout you all stuck out here, 'bout how you's plannin' to go to Harvest Hill and start anew. People get pretty talkative when they's got a gun in their face."

I felt a cold hand squeeze my innards picturing Lassiter pulling a gun on Daddy. I shoved the image away, but it did no good. It was there to stay in my brain.

"The way I figures it," said Lassiter, "you's was s'posed to hit Devil's Pass about two weeks ago. Had you come straight through, you would have. We were waitin' there for anybody to come along. Then the weather hit and we was stuck there a spell. If you'd come by when you's s'posed to, we'd have gotten you sooner." Lassiter chuckled. "But . . . " He turned to look at McCray. "Jack McCray, is it?"

McCray acted as if he hadn't been spoken to.

"Well, you brought them all down the scenic side of the mountain. Seems you had other plans."

"Why?" said Lenora. "Why would he . . . ?"

Lassiter shrugged. "When you owe people lots of money, you's get desperate. The redskin tolt us 'bout yer gamblin' debts. You owe the wrong people, McCray. They want you dead. That's why you decided to pack up and haul ass. Word 'bout folks like you travels fast, especially when somebody's willin' to pay."

Ellie slapped the ground. "What's he talkin' about, Daddy?" Her voice sounded thick and warbly as she fought back the tears I saw shimmering in her eyes. "What is he sayin'?"

Lassiter chuckled. "Yer old man's yeller, dear. He ain't gonna admit to shit." Lassiter stepped down to Mary. "How 'bout you? You got the balls to confess? Yer in on it just like he is."

That revelation hadn't been any great surprise, but it still sucked the wind out of me to learn it.

“Are you the law?” she asked.

Lassiter laughed. “Do I look like the law, honey?”

“Then I have nothing to say to the likes of you.”

“That s’posed to hurt my feelings?” He laughed but stopped abruptly. “Well, it kinda did, if I’s tellin’ you the truth.” He cleared his throat. “I’m not all bright, but I’m no idjit, either. What the redskin wouldn’t tell me, I’s able to piece together. Jack McCray gained a bounty on his head by some of those unlawful types he owed money to. When we learnt he was here from the redskin, we decided we wanted to collect it. But that damned snow kept us holed up at Devil’s Pass, waitin’. And waitin’. We was goin’ to kill all’s you, then hand over McCray and collect. Well, after talkin’ to the redskin while we waited , the plan changed.”

“Stop talking,” said McCray.

Lassiter laughed. “Found yer tongue, huh? I guess you thought if you killed them all, made it look like thieves got to you, then you could take their money and pay off your debts, then move on to Harvest Hill and start anew.” Lassiter laughed. “It was a dumb plan. Even the redskin knew that.”

“Not McCray,” said Wally, laughing.

“That’s right,” said Lassiter. “He probably thought it was the best plan since God created tits. But yer stupid plan just might work. ‘Cause, we’re thieves, and we’re goin’ to rob you and kill you. Only you won’t be alive, McCray. We will.”

Lassiter and his thugs laughed at this as if Lassiter had just unleashed the best joke any of them had ever heard. I suppose it was a joke, funny to them since we were all the punchline thanks to McCray.

I recalled the original plan that Daddy and Mr. Shumaker had come up with. It didn't seem like it would make the travel any shorter, but it sure would have been safer. It had been McCray who'd convinced them to go this route, to cut straight through the mountain. Ahote had even vouched that he could lead us along McCray's way without any incident.

And Chenona had said McCray poisoned the horses. Soon as we'd entered the woods, McCray's plan had gone into action.

Then something else triggered in my head.

I looked at Ahote. "You knew about this, didn't you?"

Ahote didn't react. I didn't know what I expected him to do. Maybe a gasp, or at least a subtle body flinch as I threw my accusation at him. I didn't get anything, which made me think I was right.

Lassiter laughed. "You's really smart, boy. Damn." Lassiter patted Ahote's head as if he were a mutt. "We might not ever have found you's if it weren't fer our friend here. He's a good guide, fer shore. I didn't know McCray had worked another deal on the side with the redskin until we's got to workin' on him. Yer daddy sure didn't know it, either. I guess McCray had promised him a better life in Harvest Hill. Flashed money and the redskin turned white. The dollar bill'll do that. Make the most loyal into a traitor."

My eyes filled with tears at the mention of Daddy. I wanted to ask Lassiter again where Daddy was but decided he wouldn't tell me. He was enjoying making us suffer. There was no other reason for him to be sharing this story, other than to torment us. If I started bawling about Daddy, he would make sure whatever his answer was would be a hurtful one.

Lassiter ruffled Ahote's dirty hair. Ahote's eyes showed no emotion to Lassiter's contact or words.

"So," said Lassiter. "We gonna steal McCray's idea. We's gonna take yer savings." He looked at Lenora. "And I'm takin' you. Ever since I saw you in that picture, I wanted you."

Lenora moaned.

My stomach felt as if a cold hand were squeezing it. "Please . . . " I shook my head.

Wally stepped forward. "You said Ken and me could get us a girl, too."

"There's two left."

"I want her," said Ken, pointing at Ellie.

"You're sick," said Wally.

"I likes what I like."

Ellie turned pale. She lowered her eyes and stared at the snow.

Wally looked at Janey. "Guess that leaves us, sweetheart. I likes them pigtails of yers."

Janey made a face. She looked away and quietly sobbed. Seeing this brought laughter out of Wally.

Jonathan pushed himself to his knees. "You have to get through me first."

Wally threw back his head and howled with laughter. "That's the idear, son. You's ain't gonna be alive to do nothin' 'bout it." Wally pointed his pistol at Jonathan.

"Hold up," said Lassiter. "Not yet. Check out the wagon. Look past the dead kid and find their loot."

Wally nodded, then headed over to the wagon.

Lassiter faced all of us again. "To be honest, I's figered when we's got here, we'd find a bunch of bodies, starved to death. We'd just come through like vultures, peckin' what we wanted. Nope." He reached around Ahote's head and patted his cheek harder than he needed to. "We's got lucky, again. Somebody up there's really lookin' out fer us. This kid's tolt us quite a fascinatin' story, redskin." Lassiter down at the top of Ahote's head. "The kid says yer woman put a curse on their folks because they ate yer baby."

This time, Ahote's eyes twitched.

"Guess they's must've been damn hungry to dig up a dead baby and eat it."

Ahote's hand clenched into a fist. Lassiter saw it, smacked Ahote on the back of the head. "Sorry to be the bearer of bad news, redskin. Guess yer baby didn't make it, so McCray and them . . . " He pointed to Mama and the Shumakers. " . . . decided not to let the meat go to waste. Oh, and from what the boy says, yer woman offed herself with an icicle to the throat to make sure what she put on them couldn't be reversed." Lassiter laughed. "Evil bitch. But I's understand it." He whistled. "The shit this boy's seen would have made my hair turn white, if it hadn't been burnt off like my face."

A tear trailed down Ahote's cheek. Though a part of me felt awful for the pain he must have been holding in, I couldn't pity him as much as I wanted to. He'd been working with McCray, which meant he had betrayed Daddy.

Lassiter leaned down to Ahote. "Tell me, is what the boy says true? Could yer woman spin a curse like that?"

Ahote nodded, then mumbled something that sounded like: "Wendigo."

"That's what she did? Wendee-go?"

Ahote said nothing more.

"Hmm," said Lassiter, standing upright. "I think we's gonna have us some fun, Ken."

Ken smiled, though there was nothing about his expression that made me think he was enjoying any of this.

Lassiter removed his pistol and lowered it to Ahote. The big man stayed on his knees, staring at the ground. He didn't even flinch when Lassiter put the barrel against the back of his head.

"Thanks, redskin," said Lassiter. "You did everything you's said you would. You brought us here, but I since I see yer family's already dead, then our deal is off."

The boom of the pistol seemed to rattle my bones. The bullet tore through Ahote's face, blowing it wide and leaving a dark gully the size of a fist between the flapping skin that had once been his nose. Blood, skull, and teeth spattered across the snow and sprayed all over Lenora. She did not get up, just remained on her knees, shaking and screaming.

Ahote pitched forward, landing on his chest. His head splashed chunky red in front of him.

Wally poked out his head from the wagon. "Who the hell's shootin'?"

Ken sighed. "Lassiter killed the Indian."

"Already?"

Ken nodded.

"Damn," said Wally. "Hate I missed it."

"Did you find anything?" asked Lassiter.

"Oh, yes, I did. All their money is in here. Just like the Indian said."

"Good. Bring it out. When yer done, we's gonna have some fun."

19.

WALLY DRAGGED OUT the trunks, letting them drop to the ground. After Ken had moved Ahote's body, leaving behind a clumpy red spatter in the snow, he joined Wally. Together, they began taking the money and putting it in sacks they'd brought with them. I saw Wally drop in the watch Daddy gave me and almost started crying again.

Lassiter watched his men work, his stiff lips stretching into an ugly smile.

"Stop," said McCray through a groan. He sounded as if he were in pain. "Can't we work out some kind of . . . trade?" He shivered.

"Trade?" said Lassiter. "Hell no. We're already takin' the girls and the money, you got nothin' else I want. I might have taken her." Lassiter nudged Mama's knee with the toe of his boot. She hissed at him, which caused him to snatch back his foot. "Jeez-us wept."

"Thar's some silverware," said Ken. "Want us to take that?"

"By all means," said Lassiter.

Mama sniffled through her groans. The silverware had belonged to Grams. It was passed down to Mama when she died. It had been in the family for a long time.

Though I could tell it broke her heart, Mama didn't bother trying to talk them out of taking it. Anger flowed through me watching them pack it up, knowing how bad it was hurting Mama. In that moment, I'd forgotten about what she'd done to my ear.

"Got an issue with us takin' yer stuff, boy?" Lassiter's voice.

At first, I wasn't sure who he was talking to. I glanced at Jonathan, saw he was looking back at me. Then I realized I was the one Lassiter had asked. I looked up at him. He was looking down at me, the loose strands of bandage rustling in the cold breeze.

"Leave my brother alone," said Lenora.

Lassiter chuckled. "Such a tough mouth on you. Can't wait to break you and make you go squealy."

"I'll die first."

"Not first," said Lassiter. "But you will eventually, when I's allow it to happen." Lassiter looked at me again. "See that Ken?"

"What?" said Ken, walking back to Lassiter. He still carried Jonathan's rifle in one hand. In the other, he carried a sack that looked weighed down and on the verge of splitting open.

"I think the kid don't like us very much."

"I bet he don't."

Lassiter feigned a gasp. "What have we done to get such ill treatment?"

Ken shrugged. "Stealin' their stuff? Takin' his sister? And his lady friend too? I can tell he likes her from the way he keeps lookin' at her."

"At who? Pigtails?"

"Nope. Red."

I glanced at Ellie. She was looking at me, her bright eyes nearly the same color as the snow.

"Oh," said Lassiter. "I see. Little lovebirds. Ain't that the sweetest you ever saw?"

Ken nodded, his eyes fixed on Ellie. "She's gonna be real sweet." He turned to me, a corner of his mouth lifting. The expression made his beard look as if it were longer on one side. "Too bad you ain't never gonna know."

Lassiter shook his head. "I don't understand the likes of you."

"I don't understand me either."

Wally approached. "I went through the wagon another again and didn't find nothin' else. We gots plenty of loot, some jewelry, and silverware."

"Struck it big?" asked Lassiter.

"Biggest we ever did."

Lassiter whistled. "Guess McCray had the right idea, after all." Laughing, he looked back at McCray. "Eatin' you up inside, ain't it?"

The three men began to laugh.

McCray was bent forward, his elbows pressed to his stomach. Groans and grumbles came from him, but I didn't think they were produced by his mouth. He really looked as if something was gnawing him under his skin from the way he shook and writhed.

I saw quick movement in the corner of my eye. Turning my head, I spotted Janey on her knees. Her hands were digging in the snow as if she were a prairie dog trying to excavate a den of rabbits. I wasn't sure what she was doing. I briefly wondered if she were trying to tunnel a way out of here.

Then with a speed I didn't know she possessed she

brandished the other pistol. It looked coated in oil from the way the snow made it gleam. The smart girl had buried it when she realized we were being visited by wayward bastards.

She had the hammer pulled back and the barrel leveled before anybody knew what she was up to.

The clack of the hammer resounded louder than the laughter, killing it. The men started to turn.

"Shit," muttered Lassiter.

The pistol spat fire with a roar that ruffled my hair. Wally's neck exploded in a cloud of red and flesh. Before he hit the ground, Lassiter had pulled his weapon and fired back at Janey. I saw sparks fly where her hand was, then the pistol soared away from her. Holding up her hand, I saw her face through the massive hole that went straight through her palm, taking off a chunk of the fleshy spot below her thumb.

Screaming, Janey pulled her injured hand close and dropped onto her side. Ellie crawled over her, trying to help but looking as if she had no idea how to begin. Janey wouldn't stop screaming, wouldn't stop swaying and rocking back and forth for Ellie to even try.

Now was the right time to go at Lassiter with the knife hidden in my belt.

While Ken went to needlessly check on Wally, Jonathan used this moment to jump to his feet. I saw where he was going. The pistol had landed a few short strides from where he had been laying. Lenora must have noticed too because she began to get up, and I felt her hands slide under me just as I started to reach for the knife hidden in my belt.

Her tugging forced my hand away from the hilt just as my fingers brushed the tip.

"Wait . . . " I started to say.

But Lassiter's gunfire cut me off. A bullet punched into the ground in front of the pistol when Jonathan was about to grab it. Dirt and snow shot back, pelting Jonathan's face. It looked as if some got in his eye. Squinting on one side, he jumped back, a hand to his eye.

This didn't look as if it was going to stop Lenora. She was determined to get the pistol and didn't seem to care if Lassiter knew. Dragging me with her, she started toward it. I couldn't get my hands behind me and now it was too late. Lassiter was on to Lenora's plan.

He pointed his gun at Jonathan. "Another step and I put one through his other eye."

Lenora didn't stop completely, but she did slow down.

Lassiter cocked the pistol. This brought Lenora to a standstill.

"There's a good girl," said Lassiter. "Stubborn as a damned ox." He walked over to where Jonathan was on his knees, his left eye covered. Lassiter peered down at him for a moment, then kicked him in the gut. Jonathan bent forward and hacked.

"Stop it!" Lenora cried.

Lassiter put his gun to Jonathan's head. "Would you rather I do this?"

She shook her head.

"Then shut up. Yer on thin ice with me, bitch. Sit down."

Lenora looked at me. The expression on her face was like a child who'd just been caught doing something she shouldn't have been. Then she sank down to her knees, shoulders slumping. What fight she'd had left in her was gone.

"You too," said Lassiter, waving his pistol at me.

I obliged, parking next to my sister. The snow began to soak through my pants. The blade of the knife was cold and stiff against my back.

Lassiter turned and looked at Ken. He was crouched over Wally, gently shaking him as if it would cause the dead man to suddenly sit up and talk about the gunshot being a close call. I knew he wasn't sitting up, though. The hollow in his throat was deep and nearly teeming with blood. His mouth was slacked open, his eyes wide and blank as they stared straight up.

"Stop, you horse's ass," said Lassiter.

Ken gave Wally another shake, then looked over his shoulder. "He's dead."

"I can see that. Ain't nobody gettin' up from that."

Ken turned, snatched the rifle up from the ground, and faced Janey. She hadn't moved from her side, her twitching hand close to her bosom. He marched toward her, lowering the rifle so the barrel was level with her head.

"Don't!" Floyd yelled. "Please, don't!"

Patty let out a squeal that might have been a plead, but I couldn't tell.

"Damn bitch," he muttered.

"Easy," said Lassiter.

"The hell you mean 'easy?' She killed Wally. I'm going to put a bullet in her. We don't need her none nohow. Wally picked her. Since he's dead, what we need her fer?"

Lassiter nodded. "In time." His dark eyes scanned

all of us. "I was content with having you all line up on your knees and blowin' your asses away. Would be quick and mostly painless. Headshots, you know. You'd know it was comin', but when it did, you wouldn't know nothing else. But now, after Pigtails over there and my darlin', Curly, I don't thinks I'm gonna be so merciful."

Lassiter looked at Lenora. "You's got to learn real quick, girlie. I'm not one to cross. You's gonna be with me for a while, and I can't have you thinkin' you's gonna get the better of me."

"I've been beaten before," said Lenora.

I looked at Lenora. That was the first I'd ever heard about that. I wasn't sure if she was lying to try and sound tough to Lassiter, or if she was confessing something that she'd kept private. I didn't think Jonathan could have ever done that to her. Not that I thought it was above such things, but had he tried something like that with Lenora, she would have made him pay for it.

Lenora straightened her back. "No amount of beatings you could give me would ever change how I feel about you."

Lassiter nodded. "Don't doubt it. Which is why I ain't talkin' about beatin's. I'm talkin' about teachin' yer ass a lesson." He pointed at me. "Ken. Grab him."

Lenora hugged my arm. "Don't you dare. Stay away from him!"

Lassiter stepped over to Lenora, raised his foot and put it on her shoulder. He shoved, throwing her back. Her hands slipped off my arm. Then he waved his pistol toward Mama. "Get the boy over there."

Ken chuckled. He gripped the back of my coat and

began to drag me toward her. I flung my arms, swinging wildly trying to strike Ken. There was no use. I was much too short to reach him.

We were closing in on Mama. She turned, saw us coming. Her lips quivered around her bloodstained teeth. She began to moan.

"Please," I said, my voice barely able to come out.

"What'd you say, boy?" asked Lassiter.

"Please!" I tried to pull away from Ken. To be holding me with one arm, his grip was firm enough that it felt like two. "Don't do this! Don't!"

I could hear the others joining in, begging Lassiter to reconsider. I think Jonathan even offered to take my place. They might as well have been yelling at the trees.

"Stop fightin'," said Ken. "It's sad, kid."

I didn't stop fighting. I bucked and jumped and writhed to no avail. Ken was too strong for me. He towered over me, his arm like a tree branch.

Mama saw how close we were to her. She began to bounce like a dog about to receive a special treat. Her stomach groaned like a tree breaking. "Hungry . . . so hungry . . . "

"What should I do about 'er hands and feet?" asked Ken.

"Leave 'er tied," said Lassiter. "Don't want 'er coming after us."

"Right."

I continued to beg, to struggle. I even tried biting Ken, but the thickness of his Confederate coat was too much for my teeth to penetrate.

We reached Mama, and he threw me down in front of her. Then he got down on a knee behind me, reached over, and grabbed my arms. I wasn't sure where he put the rifle. I figured it had to be close to him.

I tried to pull it away, but it was a useless attempt.

Lassiter laughed. "I've been listenin' to that bitch's stomach growl for a while now. I think it's time she got to get a little nibble."

Mama moaned. Then the Shumakers began to join her. I could hear Floyd praying quietly to himself, praying they don't tempt him because he knew he'd fail.

Ken laughed. Hot air that smelled rancid puffed against me. "She only got to eat an ear, Lassiter. Maybe she'd like some fangers."

Lassiter laughed. "Good idear. I'm curious to see if she'll even do it, or if they've been shoveling us horseshit for the last little bit."

Ken slapped his hand around my wrist and pulled my arm straight. I tried to keep my arm bent, but there was no battling Ken.

Mama leered at my hand. Her tongue slid across her lips, moving from one side to the other. She smacked her lips as her stomach let out another gurgle.

"The way I's figure it," said Lassiter, "if you's tellin' the truth about all this, then yer ma won't be able to resist taking a nibble off you."

Mama snarled. In a croaky voice, she said, "So . . . hungry . . . baby . . . boy . . . please . . . don't . . . hate me . . . "

I began to cry. "Don't . . . Mama, please . . . "

Ken pushed my hand forward.

My fingers rubbed across Mama's mouth. She pressed her lips in a tight line, turning her head to try avoiding my touch. I was wailing by this point, any attempts of begging had turned to incoherent blubbers. I could hear Lassiter laughing, Ken laughing, and the others shouting as my fingers brushed Mama's lips back and forth.

She seemed to be trying to resist, trying not to succumb to the hunger. Her defiance didn't last much longer. Her tongue came out like a big, purple slug, sliding across my fingertips, feeling warm and spongy.

Ken's spit sprinkled across the side of my face while he yipped and hollered like a loon. He gave me another push.

My pinky and ring fingers went into Mama's mouth.

For a brief moment, I thought she was going to spit them back out. The way her brow furrowed when my fingers passed her teeth, it looked as if she no longer wanted to eat them.

But then her teeth clamped like a trap. Pain shot up my arm. I began to scream as Lassiter and Ken cheered her on.

Mama's head shook, her teeth sinking deeper. Blood began to spurt, spilling across her nose. Her head whipped more vigorously, then shot back. She began to chew as blood spurted from the uneven stumps, slicking her face.

Ken threw me onto Mama's lap. My face mashed into her thighs. I could hear him laughing as I threw myself to the side to get away from her. I got to all fours and started to crawl, leaving a red streak in the snow as my hand dragged across. Then he kicked me in the rump and knocked me forward.

Laying on my stomach, I started to cry even harder.

20.

"WELL," SAID LASSITER. "That was shore fun."

"What we going to do now, Lassiter?" Ken asked.

"We should probably start out soon. Make some distance before nightfall." Lassiter looked up. "Those clouds shore look wicked. Probably gonna snow again."

Ken remained squatted near me. "Want me to start pluggin' 'em?"

At that point, I wished they would. I would have rather had a bullet put in my head than to endure anymore of this madness. But I somehow knew it wouldn't be that simple.

Lassiter walked toward Janey, making a wide step over Wally's supine body. "Ken, put Wally with the redskin."

"That's not right. Wally don't like 'em."

"What's it matter? He's dead."

Ken nodded. "Guess it don't matter none." He stood up with a groan, then stepped over to Wally. He gripped his ankles and began to drag him.

Lassiter reached Janey, grabbed her arm and pulled. "Come on, darlin'."

"We's takin' her wit us?"

"Hell no, Ken. She killed Wally. She's stayin'." He threw her to the ground next to Jonathan. "Grab the rope when yer done."

"We don't have much."

"We don't need much."

Ken stopped pulling Wally when the dead man's head was parallel with Ahote's feet. He let his legs drop. They landed in the snow with a heavy thump. "Be right back."

Ken stomped off toward the trees.

Floyd cleared his throat. "Whatever you're planning, please spare the children."

Lassiter chuckled. He stepped over to Lenora, resting a hand on the top of her head similar to how he'd done with Ahote earlier. "I'm not going to do anything to the children. Y'all are."

My stomach dropped. I rolled onto my side to see Lassiter. His smile was showing in the gap between the bandages.

Patty began to cry again. "No . . . "

Lassiter laughed. "Aren't y'all hungry?"

At the mention of hunger, their stomachs began to scream.

Mary stomped her feet. "Don't do this!" She turned to McCray. "Do something!"

McCray just shook his head.

"Wait," said Lassiter. He looked at Ellie. "Red's yer kid, right?"

Mary sniffed, then turned her head.

Lassiter looked at me. "You's tolt me the redskin bitch said they would *devour* their own young. But didn't you also say that McCray and his woman was munchin' on the kid in the wagon?"

I nodded.

"Well, which is it? Their own young, or any young? That don't make sense. Seems the rules are a little blurred." He rubbed his chin with a finger. "Guess I don't like the odds of not doin' this right."

"Not doin' what right?" Ken's voice made me flinch. I hadn't heard him return.

"We're ditchin' Red here too. Can't leave out the McCrays. Don't want to risk them just walkin' off with their bellies empty."

Mary, realizing what Lassiter meant, began to sob.

"What the hell, Lassiter?" said Ken. "You's said I could—"

"—I'll give you Wally's share of the loot to make it fair. You can buy yerself a girl when we get to Billstown."

Ken was quiet for a moment. "That's fair, shore."

I had never heard of Billstown, but I figured it was the kind of town that welcomed brutes like Lassiter and Ken with open arms.

Lassiter pointed at Jonathan and Janey. "Tie them together, back-to-back."

Ken nodded. He walked over to Jonathan and Janey. Jonathan had his twin sister pulled close, arms around her. She held her trembling hand off to the side. Blood dribbled from the hole. Her hand looked as if it had been painted red.

"Move it," said Ken, nudging Jonathan's hip with his boot.

"Piss off," said Jonathan.

"Big talk," said Ken.

"What are you going to do? Kill me?"

Lassiter whistled. "He's gettin' big on you, Ken."

"I see that," said Ken.

"Guess we have to start workin' on that sister of his till he decides to stop being too big fer his britches."

Patty gasped. Floyd turned to her, talking quietly. Her sobs were loud for a bit, but they began to dissipate.

Jonathan looked at Ken another moment, then slid over as Ken had instructed. Janey had to scoot to give him room.

"Was that so hard?" Lassiter asked. "Now put your backs together."

It took them longer to get in the position they wanted because of Janey's hand, but they finally were back-to-back. Ken pulled the arms behind their backs, causing Janey to cry. She hollered when he began tying the rope around their wrists.

"I bet that stings, huh?" said Ken. "I've been shot before. It ain't pleasant."

Janey took a deep breath and let it out with a groan.

Chuckling, Ken stood up. He walked over to Ellie and grabbed her arm. Her breaths turned squeaky as she shook her head. She tried to pull away, but Ken just walked on, dragging her with him. He acted as if she weren't giving him any kind of trouble.

When he reached me, he flung Ellie against me, knocking me over. I heard Lenora say something, then Lassiter laughed.

Ken ordered for Ellie and me to do the same as Jonathan and Janey. I didn't bother disputing him and sat up, putting my arms behind me. My hand throbbed, which caused my ear to throb as if the wounded parts of my body were communicating.

Ken had to force Ellie against me. Soon as I felt the firmness of her back against mine, Ken began binding us together.

"All done," he said, standing. His knees crackled as his legs straightened.

"Good. Cut their parents loose."

"Um . . . " Ken scratched his head. "You shore that's a good idear?"

"Why ain't it?"

"Well . . . don't you think they's gonna come right after us when they loose?"

"They're hungry. They don't want us."

"They might want to kill us."

McCray snorted at the mention of that.

Lassiter nodded. "I see yer point, Ken." He paced in front of Lenora a few times, then stopped. "Bonk 'em on the head a good time, then cut 'em loose. That should give you plenty of time to get away from 'em."

"What we gonna do? We gonna watch?"

"I'd like to, Ken, but . . . " He looked up at the sky. "We've run out of time for the fun. Best we get goin'."

Lassiter walked over to what was left of the rabbit. He stared down at it for a few seconds. I thought for sure he was wondering where the knife had gone to. Any moment, I expected him to turn to me and demand I hand it over. He'd seen where I had landed earlier. Surely, he'd seen the knife too.

"We should take this meat," said Lassiter. "Eat it later."

Ken was standing behind Mary, Jonathan's rifle above her head. "Sounds good." He brought the wooden stock down, hitting her on the back of the head.

Mary let out a grunt, then sunk forward. Her rump was up in the air, face on the ground. Ken leaned over, slipping out a knife from inside his boot. The blade was much longer than the one on the knife I had hidden behind my belt.

Ken repeated this process all the way down the line. By the time he had finished with Mama, Mary was starting to stir.

"Take the rope," said Lassiter. "To replace ours. It's only fair."

"Fair fer shore," said Ken, gathering it up. Then he walked over and scooped up the rabbit meat. "I'll put it in my bag when we get back to the horses."

Lassiter walked over to Lenora, pointing his gun at her. "You doin' this the easy way or hard way?"

Lenora opened her mouth to say something. Before she could, Lassiter swung down, punching her on the chin. Lenora dropped to the ground in a limp fold.

"Hard way, I guess."

Seeing him strike my sister that way filled me with fire. If I could have gotten my hands on him, I would have dug my fingers into his sockets and tugged out his eyes. But I could do nothing. My hands were tied to Ellie's. I could feel her cold skin on mine.

As Ken gathered up the sacks he and Wally had stuffed full of our belongings, snow began to drift down. I hated the fluffy dots. Hated the cold. I promised myself if I ever got out of this, I would go someplace where I never had to worry about snow.

Though my arms were taut behind my back, I could move hands a little. The ropes scratched my wrists as I tried to twist my hands. Any movement caused my ruined hand to flare up. The pain made me queasy, but I kept trying to work them under my coat.

I couldn't do it.

"What are you doing?" Ellie asked in a quiet voice.

"I have a knife . . . under my coat. If I can get it, I can probably saw the rope." The fingers I had left rubbed at the padding of the coat. Each time the nubs Mama had left behind brushed against me, I flinched. I could feel the bulge of the hilt through the fabric, teasing me.

I couldn't move my coat out of the way to grab it.

"Get it," said Ellie.

I felt her head looking around.

"I can't. My coat . . . "

I felt Ellie's fingers push mine out of the way. Her hands slipped under the flap of my coat. She was already much closer to grabbing the knife than I was. The angle she could go in, she didn't have as much working against her. I wasn't so sure she could actually reach the knife, though.

"Ow . . . " she said in a quiet voice.

"What?"

"Cut myself."

"Just leave it."

"No. I'm close."

"She's gettin' up," said Lassiter.

His voice made Ellie and me jump. She stopped trying to get the knife.

At first, I thought he was talking about Lenora. But when I looked, I saw Lenora was still out cold on the ground.

But Patty was on all fours, head swaying. Her stomach growled so hard it made her whole body shudder. The sound seemed to be what Floyd needed to hear to get him moving.

"Dad," said Jonathan. "Dad! Untie us."

Lassiter nudged Ken with his elbow. "A dollar says he tries to untie the kids and I end up shootin' him anyway."

"Yer on," said Ken, laughing. "You can afford to spare a dollar now."

"You can too," said Lassiter through a booming chortle.

"Daddy," said Janey. "Help us . . . "

Patty started crawling toward Jonathan and Janey, then paused. Her head dropped into the snow while one arm slipped over her stomach and held it. Raising her head, her mouth aimed upward, she let out an agonized wail at the sky. The tormented sound of it silenced everyone, caused Ellie to halt her attempts at grabbing the knife.

All of us just stared at her.

"It's happening again," she said. "Floyd . . . it's happening . . . "

Jonathan shook his head. "No, Mama. Fight it. Please, untie us. We'll help you . . . "

"You'll kill us!" Her voice sounded malicious, filled with spite. "You wanted to kill us before . . . "

Jonathan didn't seem to know what to say. His mouth moved but no words came out. Janey, behind him, turned her head sideways as if she were trying to see over his shoulder.

Floyd finally got to his knees. "It's happening to me . . . too."

"I'm so hungry . . . " said Patty. "It's killing me!"

"We can't . . . do it . . . " Floyd looked at Jonathan. "Son . . . we're too weak."

"Daddy," Janey cried. "Please, help us!"

"Help them!" Ellie cried.

Her hands went back to work on the knife. I felt it shift behind me. She was getting closer. I felt jittery inside as the knife began to wiggle. I felt a nick on the small of my back. I hissed.

"Sorry," said Ellie, her voice low.

I didn't care if she sliced my back to ribbons, so long as she was able to get the knife and start using it on the rope.

Ken pointed at us. "Look at 'em," he said. "They want to go help 'em!" Ken started laughing.

Lassiter laughed as well. "This is too much. But they really need to get a move on it. We're wasting more time than we have to spare."

Floyd crawled closer to Jonathan. Seeing how close he was, Jonathan leaned the other way, trying to put more distance between himself and his father.

"Stop, Dad! Stop!" Jonathan tried to scoot. Even with Janey's assistance, they weren't going anywhere. "Get away!"

Patty had caught up to Floyd and was on her way to pass him. Floyd paused, shaking his head as if doing so might jar away his cravings. He looked like a dog fresh from the pond, shaking and flinging this way and that. He even began to growl.

Seeing this caused Lassiter and Ken to stop laughing. For the first time, they showed a hint of fear. Ken leaned in, whispering something to Lassiter.

I felt the knife start to move again.

"Just get it," I said. "Don't worry about cutting me."

"I almost have it."

Patty was inches from Jonathan. Her body moved as if her ligaments had gone stiff. She twitched with each movement. Her hair draped her face, but did not cover her mouth, which was wide open. She flipped her head to fling the hair off her face.

And that was when I saw her eyes.

They had turned white. It looked as if milk had been poured into the sockets, submerging the natural color under a thick coat. Jonathan saw this as well. He began to scream.

"What is it?" Janey shouted over him. "What's wrong?"

"Their eyes! They're . . . "

Jonathan never got to finish the sentence. Patty flung herself on top of him. Her mouth went right to his neck and bit down. Her teeth sank into the hard flesh, turning Jonathan's shouts to gargled cries.

Lassiter brought his fist up to his mouth and shouted, "Oh, shit!"

Ken pointed. "She got him!"

I felt the knife slip out from my belt.

"Got it!" Ellie cried.

"Good. Can you use it?"

"Yep!"

I felt the blade turning. I hoped she could saw fast. I doubted her speed would be very swift, though, from the way she would have to hold the knife.

I dared another look at the Shumakers. Janey had turned her head in another attempt to see her brother. "Jonathan! What's happening? Jonathan!"

Floyd was back on all fours, moving again like a coyote scouting out wounded prey. That was what his kids had become, what we all had become, really.

Easy prey waiting for a merciful kill.

Patty pulled back her head, a bundle of Jonathan's flesh clamped between her teeth. It peeled down, ripping his throat open wide and dumping blood as if it were being dropped from a bucket. With the flesh gone, I saw muscles and things that looked like skinny rope underneath. Jonathan twitched and jerked, making sounds as if he were choking. His feet kicked at the ground, digging into the snow.

While Patty chewed, she reached out, tearing his shirt open. Jonathan's wide eyes followed her movements, his mouth open as if still trying to communicate his pleas.

Janey jerked and thrashed, kicked her feet. It looked as if she were trying to get up. The rope kept her bound to Jonathan's limp weight. She wasn't going anywhere, which meant she could do nothing to thwart her father when he crawled over top of her.

"Forgive me, sweetheart . . . " His voice sounded like two stones rubbing together. His eyes were lost behind the milky shield between the lids. Mouth open, he dropped his head and vanished out of my line of sight.

Janey began to shriek and tremor as sounds like paper tearing blended with them. Blood spurted and pumped in thick crimson arcs on the other side of Janey's shoulders.

I looked over and saw Mama was sitting up. She was leaned back, hands flat on the snow as she watched the Shumakers feast upon their children. Her tongue dangled from her mouth while she panted like a spent dog trying to cool himself down.

Her head turned and she locked eyes on me. I jerked back as if she had stricken me.

Ellie let out a gasp. “What?”

“Move faster, Ellie!”

“I’m trying!”

I could feel the knife was free, could feel the up-and-down movements as she tried to saw the blade through. I looked over at Lassiter and Ken. Gone was the amused merriment. They watched with shared expressions of fear and disgust.

“Maybe uh . . . ” Ken scratched his head. “Maybe we should get outta here, Lassiter.”

Lassiter nodded. “Good idear.” He put his gun away. He picked up Lenora and carried her as if she were his bride and they were stepping over the threshold of their home to begin their new life. Lassiter gave a glance back at us. “It’s been fun, but we’ve got to be on our way.”

When Ken had gathered up everything, he hurried to catch up to Lassiter. They rushed into the trees, vanishing between a pair of thick trunks. Within a few seconds, they were gone.

Janey’s shrieks turned to frenzied wails, bringing all our attention toward her. Ellie stopped moving. I felt her head turn.

Floyd was up on his knees, swinging his arms. With each rotation came a moist punching sound that sent blood and scraps of flesh flying. His hands didn’t come up after a few turns. Jutting his chin, the veins in his neck bulged like mole trails on the ground as he pulled. There was an awful ripping, and his hands came up with balls of bloody flesh. He looked at the tatters in his hands, smiling behind the smeared beard of blood on his mouth. Then he began shoving the food into his mouth, barely chewing what was in there before shoveling more in.

Janey no longer made any sounds.

Jonathan had stopped moving. Patty's face was buried halfway into his stomach while she ate. His innards formed a mound around the sides of her head, caking her hair in stringy bits and blood.

I checked on Mama again. She had turned around to face me, her eyes a white film that robbed her of the last of her humanity. She was something different now, something savage and wicked.

"Mama?" I said.

Her head tilted, mouth twitching into something that might have been a smile.

"Just stay over there," I said. "Don't come near me!"

The crunching and glugging sounds of the Shumakers' feast nearly drowned out my voice. It seemed to reverberate off the trees, coming in all directions and growing louder by the second.

"I almost got it," said Ellie.

She was right. I could tell some of the tension in the rope had slackened, though it was still too tight for me to pull my hands loose.

Mama got to her feet, swaying. She reached up to her head, rubbing the welt that caused a hillock in her hair. She lowered her head and examined the blood dripping from her fingers. She sniffed it a few times, then began to lick it off.

I averted my eyes, looking down so I didn't have to watch my mother suckle her own blood.

And that was when I noticed the McCrays were gone.

Their spots on the logs were empty. The depressions in the snow from where they landed were vacant. How long that had been the case, I had no idea. I hadn't so much as even glanced at them since all this began. I figured they had taken off before Lassiter and Ken had. Maybe they'd even stolen the men's horses. Either way, I was glad to be rid of them.

I heard another juicy ripping sound and turned to see Patty had torn open Jonathan's pants, exposing his genitals. Or what was left of them. All he had between his legs was a bloody mound covered in bite marks.

Checking on Mama, I saw she was looking at me again. She took a step forward. I involuntarily leaned back.

The sawing at my wrists stopped. For a moment, I thought I might be free. When I tried to pull my hands apart, they wouldn't budge. The rope was still there, intact.

"Ellie?" I asked. "Why'd you stop?"

Ellie screamed.

Then I heard raspy growls and chomps from behind me, causing Ellie's screams to rise in pitch and fervor.

Hot liquid spattered against the back of my head. It trickled down from my brow into my eyes, turning my vision a faded red hue.

Blood.

The McCrays hadn't fled after all.

21.

MY HANDS WEREN'T LOOSE, but I still yanked and pulled with all I had. If I could get to my feet, I might have been able to drag Ellie away from her parents before it was too late.

No matter how hard I tried, I wasn't strong enough to hardly lift her an inch. We dropped back down. Ellie let out a grunt that turned wild as more growls came at her. I heard clacking teeth, clothes tearing, and began to smell a cold coppery scent in the air. During the pauses of these sounds came the soggy cadence of chewing. Whenever that ceased, Ellie would start to scream again as the biting and gashing returned.

"Ellie!" I yelled, but there was no use.

She was being eaten alive like Jonathan and Janey, and I could do nothing about it.

The knife. Where was the knife?

I bent my wrists and reached my hands up, feeling a sharp sting on the tip of my forefinger. Ellie still had it. No longer caring to be careful, I gripped the blade and pulled down. The knife came free. I almost dropped it because of my slippery grip caused by my blood.

Holding it by the backside of the blade, I began

sliding the sharp side up and down on the rope between my wrists. It was slow going, *very* slow going, but I wasn't about to give up.

"Billy?"

I looked up at the sound of Mama's voice, not reducing my speed with the knife for a second. She looked down at me, her white eyes wide. Tears leaked down her cheeks, cutting lines through the blood on her face.

"I . . . " Mama's head dipped to the side. "I can't . . . stop myself . . . "

"I know, Mama."

"It hurts." She patted her stomach. Her fingers were arched and stiff. "Hurts here."

I kept sawing. I could feel flakes from the rope sprinkling onto my hand while I worked.

Mama shambled closer. Her feet dragged through the snow. Off to her side, the Shumakers crouched over their children, chewing on them like vultures.

"I don't . . . " Mama gulped. "Don't want to do this. I love you, Billy-boy."

Mama turned watery in my vision. I blinked the tears away and she was clear again. "I love you too, Mama."

"I can't get myself under control." Mama stood at my feet, the toes of her boots nudging the bottoms of mine. "I'm just so . . . hungry. And I can't stop myself from . . . eating you."

I kept sawing. I could feel the tightness between my wrists starting to slacken. Ellie barely made any sounds behind me, other than an occasional gasp or weep that were barely perceptible above the chomping.

Mama started to lean over, reaching out her arms. “I’m so sorry, honey. I just need to . . . eat.”

I could suddenly move my hands. There was still some rigidity, so I pulled my hands in opposite directions as hard as I could. What remained of the rope snapped. I pulled my arms around to the front of me, switched the knife around, and gripped the hilt in my left hand. My right hand was useless to me now from the missing fingers.

I rolled to the side as Mama grabbed at me. Her hand just missed my ankle as I pulled it away.

“Noooo,” Mama said through a moan. “Don’t do this to me . . . ”

“Stay back,” I said, getting to my feet. I glanced down at Ellie and quickly looked away. The glimpse of blood and bone nearly made my legs fold. “God . . . ”

Mama came forward, reaching for me. I pushed her away. She stumbled back a few steps, then looked at me as if I’d hurt her feelings. Opening her arms, she came at me again. It looked as if she were coming in for a big hug. I stepped to the side, avoiding her. She slipped in the snow and almost fell. Turning to face me, the hurt on her face was even stronger.

“Billy,” she said. “Please . . . let me . . . ”

I pointed the knife at her. “I don’t want to hurt you, Mama. Just stop it. Please? Stop. Those men took Lenora.”

Mama turned her head, looking around as if she didn’t know what I was talking about.

I pointed toward the trees. “They left. They probably haven’t gotten far. We need to go get her back.”

Mama stood there, her mouth hanging open. Bits

of snow clung to her hair as it sprinkled down around us. "Lenora?"

Nodding, I said, "Yes. Lenora. They took her. They're going to . . . hurt her. We have to—"

She ran at me. Hollering, I stepped to the side again, but not quite quick enough. Mama spun around, hissed, and slammed against me. The impact knocked me out of her grip. As she tried to grab me, her feet tangled together. She fell. Her side whammed the ground, throwing up clumps of snow.

Her head bounced off the log I had been sitting on before Lassiter and his goons showed up.

Mama went limp.

I stood there, looking down at her motionless form. "Mama?"

No answer. No movement. The only sounds were the soft squelches of chewing combined with the heavy putters of nose breathing.

"Muh-Mama?"

Still no indication I had spoken to her. She lay on her side, her back to me. Her mussed hair had fallen over her face, blocking it from my view. I couldn't tell if she were breathing or not. I didn't want to get any closer to see for sure, either. I stared, looking for any hints of fog forming from her breaths. Any hints of flickering hair from being breathed on.

I saw none.

"Mama . . . ?" My voice sounded thick and quivery. Tears welled in my eyes. Before I could even begin to wipe them away, they spilled down my face in steady rivulets. I stood there, bawling as I would have as an infant. Knowing this caused me to think of Chenona's infant and that brought on even heavier sobs.

I don't know how long I stood there crying like that. Could have been a few seconds, could have been several minutes. But the sobbing stopped as sudden as it had started. One moment, I was nearly hysterical and the next I wasn't crying at all. My chest felt sore and tight. My eyes burned. I was exhausted and somehow more alert than I had been all day.

And I was angry. So angry. I shook all over with a rage I had never felt before in all my life, nor have I felt it since then. My vision turned red, and my thoughts snuffed out like a candle flame.

I turned and looked at Ellie. She was on her back, arms behind her making her stomach jut. Her clothes had been ripped wide to expose her belly. What was left of it was a mushy pile of brown and red that McCray continued to shove his face into. Each time he dived in, his head shook, and I could hear awful glugging sounds.

He lifted his head up, smiling and moaning with a mouthful of food.

I stabbed him in the back of the neck. The blade ripped straight through and tore through the front. I had to grip the hilt with both hands, ignoring the flashes of pain from my missing fingers, to pull it loose.

I hadn't planned to do it. There had been no prior thought to my actions. I watched it play out like a spectator, just as shocked and surprised as McCray seemed to be.

McCray, hand to his throat, coughed and choked. Clumps of meat spilled down his chin. Blood flowed through the cracks of his fingers. His white eyes peered at me. A corner of his upper lip lifted, baring teeth. A part of him seemed irate about what I'd done while another part almost seemed to be delighted.

He looked as if he might charge at me. So I stepped back, readying myself with the knife in my left hand.

McCray coughed again, then fell over. He made a lethargic attempt to reach for me before his arm dropped to the ground. He didn't move again.

I turned toward Mary, expecting to find her ready to tear me apart for what I did to her husband. But she hadn't even noticed. She'd been too busy gnawing at the fleshy part of Ellie's bare thigh. She'd chewed a large hole through the meat. A chunk of bone showed between the bloody nubs of deep flesh.

Since she was too busy being distracted by the eating of her daughter, I walked right up to her and punched the knife into her throat as well. Her body jerked rigid, and she sat up so fast that I started to fall back. I kept a hold of the knife, though, so when I fell, I ripped the blade right through the front of her throat. My back smacked the ground. A chunk of neck bounced off my chest, then blood splashed the hollow of my throat. It felt warm and thick as it oozed over my skin. The heat didn't last long before it cooled to a chilly paste.

Mary, on her knees, patted the ditch in her throat. Blood showered her hands. It looked as if she were trying to catch it by the handful and shove it back in the open space only for it to pour back out. She did this for a few seconds before her movements began to weaken. Soon after that, she fell across McCray's back. I stared at her, waiting to see what she would do next. I quickly realized she wasn't in any condition to anything but lie there.

Another one, dead.

By my hands.

And I didn't feel a thing. Not even a hint of remorse for killing two people. See, I knew that they weren't really people, not anymore. That part of them died the moment they took that first bite of Chenona's baby. Even before the hex was on them, they had betrayed their own souls.

Still holding the knife, I sat up. I tried to shake the blood off my hands, but it was already freezing to me. The falling snow adhered to it, quickly melting. It softly sizzled in the spots that were still a little warm.

I got to my feet. The surge of anger I had felt was starting to dwindle, but it hadn't faded entirely. I had two more to do, so I needed to get to it, then I had to figure out how I was going to get Lenora back.

I turned around, not bothering to have the knife ready to stab anything. From the McCrays, I had become a tad spoiled in thinking that they all would be too occupied to notice what I was up to. But I was wrong.

Floyd was running straight at me, roaring.

His white eyes were narrowed, his brow pressed downward and dripping stringy bits of flesh. His teeth were streaked in red, as was the rest of his body. His balding head looked as if it had been painted in crimson mud.

I glimpsed all this in the moment right before he rammed into me.

I felt my feet lift off the ground. I swung the knife down, not sure what I would hit, if anything. To my surprise, the blade slammed down in his back. Floyd let out a howl, then tossed me over his shoulder. The world began to spin as I tumbled down his back. I didn't stop rolling when I hit the ground. Snow splashed all over me, stinging my eyes and cheeks.

I came to a stop on my back. Staring up, I tried to get the sky to stop spinning. Snow fluttered down into my eyes. Floyd's growls and screams came from off to the side of me. I turned my head, and it seemed to take my vision a moment to catch up with the movement.

Floyd was on his feet, turning circles while slapping at his back. The knife jutted from between his shoulder blades like a lever. He had long, gangly arms, but they still couldn't reach it.

I pushed myself to my knees. I checked on Patty, thinking she was probably going to come at me as well. I found her still by Jonathan, chewing at a mound of bloody mush in her palm. Her wild eyes turned every which way as if they were trying to dislodge themselves from inside her head. I figured if they somehow did, they would probably dash off in two directions.

Floyd stopped trying to get the knife. His focus centered on me. His mouth twitched a few times, then he charged at me again. His arms spun, hands locked into place with his fingers ready to gouge. I knew I had already wasted too much time watching him and should have gotten up and started to run. There was no way I would be able to now. He'd catch me before I managed to turn around.

To prove this, Floyd suddenly leapt, closing a wide berth of the gap in one motion. His feet slapped the ground. Then they shot out from under him. His legs swung back, bringing his upper torso down to the ground. He landed on his front, sliding the remaining distance toward me. His chin dug a path through the snow. He came to rest inches from my hands.

Floyd's eyes tilted upward to look at me. He snarled.

I jabbed both my thumbs in each of his eyes. It was harder to do than most would imagine. It took a lot of effort to get his eyes to go back, but once they started to move, they didn't stop until my thumbs were all the way in. I could feel them, burrowed next to the orbs, pushing them against the socket and mashing them. My fingers were spread out on either side of his head like antlers. Well, one side was. The other side looked as if a hunter had blown off some of the antlers while trying to ping a deer.

Gloppy blood spat against my hands, warming them with sticky heat. Screaming, Floyd kicked his feet and punched the ground like a toddler throwing a fit. I went to pull out my thumbs from his sockets, but they wouldn't budge. The squished eyes held them there.

I gave them a hard yank. Floyd's neck stretched, causing his screams to change pitch. My thumbs remained embedded where his eyes used to be.

I checked on Patty.

She was up and coming my way, blood dripping from her fingertips and leaving red dots along the snow next to her tracks.

Now, it was my turn to scream.

I yanked and yanked, but my thumbs stayed buried in the goop of Floyd's eyes. Each pull I attempted elicited a scream of pain from Floyd. It didn't stop him from trying to bite me, though. His mouth snapped, teeth clacking together. He was nowhere close to actually biting me, but I still jumped and flinched as if he might.

Patty was only a few steps away. She paused to scoop up a rock that was big enough to fill her hand. She brushed the snow off it.

Carrying the uneven rock above her head, she walked over to me.

I dug my boots into the ground and pulled. My rump lifted off the ground. Floyd slid closer to me, groaning the whole way. But my thumbs hardly even slid an inch. His mouth was close enough to munch now, so I had to spread my legs to avoid his gnashing teeth. If he were to slide any closer, he would be able to sink his teeth into an area I very much wanted to keep intact.

Patty, standing over me, reared the rock back. She swung down. I could feel the wind of the swing before the rock even came close to my face. I whipped my head to the side and dropped. Doing so hurt my arms since they remained embedded in Floyd's eyes. I felt the air of the rock just passing my face. The wet sleeve of her coat brushed my cheek.

Then the rock whacked Floyd's forehead, cracking it open and tearing off a chunk. The force of the hit knocked his head back so hard, his neck snapped. My thumbs plopped free. I rolled backward, flipping onto my stomach. Holding up my hands, I examined my thumbs. Other than being slicked in red gunk, they seemed fine. I was able to wiggle them, so I didn't think they were broken.

Patty began to shriek. I looked up and saw she had crouched next to her husband, holding her hands above him as if afraid touching him might cause more damage. I could tell she wanted to do something but had no idea what could be done. She realized, as did I, that there was nothing that would help Floyd right now. The back of his head rested on his back, making it appear as if a face had sprouted there—a face that was spurting blood and leaking chunks of brain and skull.

Patty dropped onto her rump, letting her arms fall in her lap. She stared at the rock clutched in her hand, sobbing. "We . . . " She sniffed, sobbed. She turned, looking past me so she could see her children. The sight of them made her bottom lip pucker and quiver. She faced me again. The sadness on her face twisted into a scowl. "We belong in Hell!"

She brought the rock up with both hands. For a moment, I thought she meant to throw it at me. I threw up an arm to shield myself. But her momentum went in the opposite direction, bringing the lumpy stone toward her own head. It smashed through her skull, collapsing her head inward. The rock stopped going about halfway in, killing her screams. She turned toward me. Head bobbing, blood trickling down her face, she somewhat smiled.

Then she dropped on her back, arms and legs splayed wide.

I stared at her for a long time. I didn't realize I'd been holding my breath until my lungs began to burn. I let it out in a rush, pulling in a deep breath that tasted vaguely of raw meat. The snow was coming down heavier now, fat fluffs of white that spattered on Patty's chest. It wasn't long before it began to spread a light dusting across her and Floyd.

I got to my feet. I stood there, wobbling for a spell before I trusted myself to walk.

"Bu . . . Billy?"

I spun around. The voice had been faint, garbled. I looked at Mama first. She still lay on her side, facing away from me. The snow had piled from her shoulder down to her leg. She hadn't budged even a smidgeon.

I scanned the carnage. Some of it, I had caused, but the rest had been put into motion by Lassiter. He had Lenora. I knew if I planned to go after them, I would need to leave very soon. I doubted they were traveling extremely fast thanks to the snow. Most likely, they'd set up camp before long, once they were a comfortable distance from here.

I waited to see if I would hear my name another time. When I was about to chalk it up to my own imagination, I heard it again.

I looked down at Ellie.

Her eyes were narrow slits, but I could tell she was looking at me. There were teeth marks in her throat, spread across her bloody skin like bird tracks in the snow. Her coat and undershirt had been torn in half, exposing her flesh underneath. I would have looked away to give her the privacy she deserved, but there was nothing there to see anymore. It had been gnawed and peeled, flattened to a meaty pulp around the bare areas of her chest and ribs.

Her arms were out by her sides, elbows slightly bent. The sleeves had been ripped through, as had the skin underneath. Strands of frayed flesh ringed the holes left behind by mouths. I saw hints of bone at the bottom of the sinewy mess inside.

"It . . . doesn't hurt . . . " Ellie said. She took a

breath that caused her chest to flutter. When she exhaled, a whistling noise came from the holes in her throat.

"No," I said in a quiet voice. Getting on my knees beside her, I took her hand in mine. It was colder than anything I'd ever touched before. I knew she had passed, but her mind just didn't know it yet. Her body had already moved on.

Ellie gulped. "I can't . . . believe this is how it ends."

I stared at her, fighting back the tears. I couldn't believe it either. It wasn't fair. None of us asked for this, especially not Ellie. She was stuck between awful, dishonest parents, only to have her demise come about because of them. It wasn't fair at all.

"Pray . . . with me?" Ellie asked.

I swallowed. Then I shook my head. "I can't, Ellie."

"Please . . . ?"

I didn't want to talk to God. I was too angry, and the words I had to say wouldn't be the right thing for Ellie's last words to hear. But I knew, even as a kid, it was Ellie's final request. She wanted to slip away hearing somebody talk to God. It would comfort her in a moment when very little could.

"Okay," I said.

"Th-thank you." She closed her eyes. Her mouth turned into something like a smile.

Turned out, I didn't need to worry about what I would say to God. Ellie died before I even got the chance to utter one divine syllable.

After a few minutes, I got back to my feet. All the rage and anger that had kept me moving on instincts that I didn't know I had quickly left me. Doing so seemed to sap me of my strength. I wanted to lie down, to rest. But I knew if I did, I wouldn't get back up. I would be buried under the snow and freeze to death.

That didn't seem like such a bad way to go.

But Lenora needed me. There was nobody else to do it. Nobody was coming for us. Before Lassiter showed up, there was still a silent hope that Daddy would find us help and ride in to save the day. Now I knew that possibility would only remain a fantasy. We were alone out here, Lenora and me. Nobody was left to help us.

Then I saw Mama. She lay there, the snow trying to cover her. A gust of wind came on, ruffling her hair and stirring her coat. Puffs of snow blew off her in a cloud.

I walked over there and collapsed next her, the tears I'd been holding back ripping through me. I wrapped my arms around her and held her tight against me, sobbing into her chest. I cried like that until I no longer had a voice left to yell out with. When that happened, I silently clucked and moaned. Eventually, the tears dried up.

But I didn't let go of her. I continued to squeeze her, just as I used to when a nightmare shocked me awake and sent me hollering for her in the middle of the night. She would barge into my room, sit on the edge of the bed, and hold me the way I was holding her until I had calmed down.

I prayed. Something I couldn't do for Ellie, I did for myself. It was a selfish prayer. I prayed to feel Mama's arms holding me one more time. I should have prayed that I would be able to save Lenora from whatever Lassiter had planned. But all I wanted in that moment was my mama back.

And He must have been listening that time. Because that was what I got. Mama's arms moved up my back, pulling me close. She squeezed me back. I heard her take a breath.

"Mama?" I said, lifting my head.

Her snarling mouth filled my vision as she moved in for a bite.

"So . . . hungry . . . "

22.

MAMA'S TEETH SCRAPED my chin as I pulled my head away. My face lit up with a cluster of stings. I tried to pull away from her, but my arms were trapped behind her and her hold on me was strong.

"Hungry . . . " she said through a snarl.

"Mama, stop!"

I bucked, shifting my weight to the right. My legs went to the left and I started to drop. Mama let out a startled yelp as she came with me. The way we fell, I figured I was going to land on my back with Mama coming down on top of me. Had that happened, I probably wouldn't be here to write this tale. But as it so happened, we came down on our sides, facing each other.

Mama's grip loosened, so I took that moment to roll away from her.

I started to get up. Her hand snatched my ankle and yanked me to the ground. Before I could try to get back up, I was pulled back.

"Stop!" I yelled.

I groped and slapped at the ground as I slid across the snow in reverse. I stole a glance over my shoulder. In my jarred vision, I saw Mama walking toward the fire. Her mussed hair bounced and flung around her shoulders. She pulled me with one hand while the other swung out to the side of her. I tried to grab hold of anything. My fingers couldn't find purchase on the snow and glided right across.

We reached the fire. The flames had dulled to weak flickers and black smoke. Mama nudged the ashy mound with her foot. Ashes scurried into the air like lightning bugs, blinking off whenever they touched snow. She gave it another nudge with her foot. A tongue of fire lashed out from under a scorched log, curling around it. It flapped as it grew, enveloping the log in crackling heat.

I jerked my leg back. Though Mama stumbled back a couple feet, her grip still held. I grabbed a handful of snow and threw it at her. It spattered against her back. She didn't even seem to notice. Still holding my leg, she leaned over and grabbed another log. Without being careful, she tossed it onto the fire. Embers misted upward, fanning around Mama. The fire burst to life with a huff of warmth that I felt on my face. It was hard to ignore how good it felt, even in my situation.

"Stay," said Mama. She dropped my leg.

Without delay, I started to get up. Mama stepped in front of me, swinging. Throwing up my arm in defense, I saw her cast iron pan right before it clanged against my left shoulder. It felt like I had been kicked by a mule and flung me just as far as one might.

I landed a few feet away, stunned by the pain shifting through my body. My left arm had gone completely numb. I tried to make it move, twitch, anything, but it was as if it wasn't there at all. With my only other option being an arm with a mangled hand, I was down to none.

Mama set the pan over the flames just as she would have when she was still able to cook breakfast for all of us. I heard sizzles and pops as the ice casing the iron began to thaw and drip into the shivering flames.

Mama marched past me, her insipid eyes aimed forward. Looking over my shoulder, I saw she was making her way over to the Shumakers. I knew what she wanted soon as I spotted Floyd. The knife hilt extended from the middle of his upper back. She was going to snatch it, for sure.

But then she surprised me by walking past him. She made her way to the wagon, pausing at one of the trunks that had been busted open on the ground. She rummaged around the scattered contents and found a pouch. I could tell from where I was it was a spice pouch.

So that meant . . .

I looked at the pan.

She was going to cook me. First, she would kill me, or at least I figured she would. I hoped the strategy wasn't my being cooked alive. Then I thought of something else—Chenona's baby. That was her plan. She was going to prepare me the same way they'd prepared the baby.

I tried my arm again. It still wouldn't move, but at least I could feel something like sand trying to work its way through my veins.

I looked over my shoulder and almost cried out when I saw Mama jerk the knife from Floyd's back. A line of blood scattered across her midriff. She ran the flat side of the blade over her tongue, lapping off the blood clinging to it.

"Mama!" I yelled. "Don't do this!"

Mama started toward me. Her lips trembled over her teeth. No words came from her mouth, only raspy moans and low growls. There didn't seem to be anything left of my mother inside that thing anymore. She was something else entirely, something coldblooded.

Wendigo.

Ahote had said it, and though I hadn't ever heard it uttered before that moment, I somehow knew he was exactly right.

But it didn't really matter what in the hell she was. She was going to cook me and eat me. I had to stop her.

How would I do that? I wondered. With no arms. Well, with only a partial arm that was operational. My left arm felt like a sandbag had been attached to my shoulder. It swung uselessly by my side as I got to my knees.

I looked at the cast iron pan. I could just faintly see a cinder glow was spreading through it because of the heat. I checked on Mama again. She was only a couple yards away. She'd be on me with that knife in a matter of seconds.

I already knew what my plan was even before the idea materialized in my brain. It was a terrible idea, but I didn't allow myself to dwell on that. If I had, I probably would have dithered, and that would have allowed Mama the few seconds she needed to get to me.

I jumped to my feet and ran toward the fire. Mama let out a growl behind me. I heard the slaps of her feet on the snow as she started to chase. Though

I was much closer to the fire, Mama and I reached it at the same time.

Reaching out with my gnarled hand, I slapped it on the handle of the pan. My skin sizzled and turned gooey, stretching across the iron and hardening. Screaming, I yanked the pan away from the fire and turned, swinging my arm with my hand melted to it.

The flat bottom struck Mama's face with a clamor that reverberated up my arm. Smoke hissed from the other side of the pan, blending with her muffled scream. Mama bent over, but the pan remained glued to her face from the melted flesh. My hand ripped free, leaving a flap of my skin attached to the handle like a fleshy flag.

I landed on my back, gazing up at Mama. She held the handle with both hands, tugging at the pan. By and by, it began to wiggle. I heard a sound like tearing fabric. Then the pan broke free with a loud rip. Mama's face was gone, save a skeletal visage coated in tacky red. The rest was stuck to the bottom of the pan like a tatty mask, the other side painted in blood as if it were glue.

Mama's jaw dropped as she unleashed an awful scream. Her eyes rolled and spun this way and that. It looked as if they might drop out of the sockets without anything to hold them there anymore.

Seeing Mama this way caused me to sob again. I knew her intentions had been to do severe harm, but she was still my mother. And I had done that to her. The others, I had felt nothing at all, but with Mama, I felt as if I were being crushed.

Mama let out another scream before suddenly dropping backward. She landed on the fire, smothering it. Her back folded over the mound of sticks and logs. Smoke began to eddy from each side of her, then flames began to slither out like snakes. They curled around her hips, igniting her coat with a *whoosh!*

Within seconds, her whole body was enveloped in fire.

While I lay there bawling, I began to smell the odor of burnt hair and another odor that reminded me of Chenona's baby.

That was because, I realized, Mama had still been holding the spice bag when she landed on the fire. The flakes had spilled all over her.

23.

I DIDN'T ALLOW myself much room to mourn. I figured there would be plenty of time for that later, if I were still alive to do it at another time. My hand was in rough shape. Not only was it missing fingers, but a large strip of my flesh had been torn off to reveal the God's design underneath. It was red and wiry, sticky with blood. The cold seemed to make the pain worse. Each time snow drizzled onto it, a flurry of pain ripped through my arm.

I used the knife to cut off a patch of Jonathan's shirt. I avoided any prolonged looks at his condition. In the quick glimpses I got, I saw he might have been in even worse shape than Ellie. I didn't look over at Janey once. I felt a little guilty for it, but not enough that I could convince myself I needed to see what had been done to her.

If I had the strength, or time, I might have buried all of them and said a small prayer over their graves. But I couldn't take any longer than I already was. Bandaging my wounded hand with a hand that wasn't my dominant one took up a lot of time. It was even more difficult from how sore my arm was after Mama's pan assault.

I did a good job not glancing at her as well, unless

I needed to. The peeks I got of her showed me plenty of charred skin and blackened appendages. The odor of cooking flesh became easy to ignore after a little bit. But nothing could distract me from the sounds of simmering flesh, the way it bubbled and popped in the heat.

I held up my hand to inspect my doctoring skills. They were poor. The compress barely held together, but I supposed it was better than nothing, if barely.

The temperature seemed to have fallen even more since the snowing picked up. Plus, I was exhausted and couldn't seem to get warm. I felt lousy for it, but I took Jonathan's coat. It didn't have much blood on it, and it hung low, which meant it covered more of my small frame. The sleeves were so long, my hands vanished inside them, for which I was grateful to have them shielded from the bitter cold.

I slipped the knife back into my belt. I looked around for something else to take that could be used as a weapon. Other than some wood from the broken trunks or sticks, I found nothing. I was tempted to hunt out a rock like Patty had done, but I also didn't want to lug it around. The knife would have to do.

As ready as I was ever going to be, I set out. I had no idea what time it was because Wally had taken Daddy's watch. Judging by what daylight managed to seep through the canopy of dark clouds, I ascertained that it was probably past dinnertime. Suppertime was a couple hours away. Most likely, Lassiter would stop for the night soon.

I doubted they'd gotten very far in the snow. Plus, they were hauling Lenora with them, and God only knew how many horses. Their trek would be even harder now, especially with Wally and Ahote dead and unable to assist.

That would work well for me, though. It shouldn't take me very long to catch up to them. I had no idea what I would do once I did, though. I figured I should come up with some details to add to my plan, other than rescuing Lenora. Strict details that I would have to abide by no matter what.

But I could come up with nothing.

I followed their horses' tracks on the path we had been taking weeks ago, going where we had intended to travel much sooner. I was alone. When I started this journey, I was with a party—with my family. Mama, Daddy, and Lenora. All of us were still together. Now, it was just me.

I would make sure it didn't stay that way. I was going to get Lenora back. And when I did, we would make Lassiter tell us what he did with Daddy. I was sure the answer was one we wouldn't want to hear, but it was something that needed to be told.

Still, I had no strategy. Not even an inkling of an idea about what to do if I caught up to them. I doubted it would be very difficult to locate them, so long as I kept moving. I would catch up to them eventually. How long it would take was up in the air.

I needed a good, solid plan of action, though.

And I needed to come up with it fast.

I'm not sure how long I walked because I barely have any memory of the journey. I moved without thought, one step at a time, putting distance behind me bit by bit. The further I went, the darker the woods became. Shadows filled empty spaces all around me, making it impossible to see much off the road. The gray clouds almost looked black, so I figured I was moving upward since they seemed much lower than they had before. And the wind was brutal, whipping me with snow, flinging my clothes against me.

A few times, I thought I might have heard wolves, but I realized it was the wind howling like a banshee all around me. But it carried something else with it, something that was hard to distinguish at first but soon became clear.

Voices.

They were faint and indistinct, but I had gotten to know Lassiter well enough to recognize his tone. I thought I also heard Lenora yelping or hollering. I couldn't tell if she was just being lippy to them, or if she were in pain.

I picked up my pace and rushed to where the road turned to the left. To my right was a steep ridge that nearly went straight down. Trees were spread all through it, the branches close enough together that they looked woven together.

The scent of woodsmoke drifted through the wind. I was close.

A few minutes later, I saw where the tracks moved to the left, leaving the road and entering the woods. There was a small path the horses had made through the trees. Off in the distance, I could see plumes of smoke rising in the air. The flames painted the trees in jittering orange.

I thought about taking the same way in they had, then decided against it. If they were to walk back this way for any reason, they would see my footprints. So I went into the woods a bit further back, moving as slow and quiet that I could. I figured the wind would hide most of any sounds I might make, but I wasn't about to bank on it hiding them all.

I made my way through the trees, careful with my steps so I wouldn't step on anything that crunched. Surprisingly, I did okay.

I came upon a stream splitting the sections of land. It wasn't very wide, but it was deep, with the water reaching about halfway up the dirt walls. The water looked like dark, trembling glass. Though I was freezing, I was thirsty. Getting down on the ground, I leaned my head over the edge. My mangled ear began to throb. Ignoring the pain, I stuck my face into the cold rush, gasping into the flowing water. After the shock faded, I opened my mouth and let the water flow inside. I took three good gulps, then forced myself to lift my head. If I guzzled much more, it might make my belly sick.

The water ran down my face, dribbling off my chin. I let out a deep breath, then shook my head to get off the rest. My face hurt from how much the cold air stung now that I was wet. Blinking water out of my eyes, I turned my head and almost shouted.

Ken was standing a few yards to my right on the other side of a horse.

"Go on," said Ken, patting the horse on the neck.

The horse let out a snort, then lowered its head to the water. Like me, it began to slurp.

How he hadn't noticed me, I didn't know. I was thankful that he hadn't. If he looked to his left, though, he might spot me. Or maybe not. It was hard to say for sure, from how heavy the snow was coming down and how much the wind seemed to be slinging the white debris all over. Not taking any chances, I remained as still as I possibly could. I kept my eyes locked on him.

While the horse lapped up water, Ken slipped out his penis and began to piss. Closing my eyes, I listened to him sigh as the heavy torrent pounded the stream. Though I couldn't see anything, it was almost as bad as watching him do it. I was grateful he hadn't decided to handle those matters while I had my face submerged in the water.

His piss slowed to a trickle, then it ended entirely.

"That's enough water," he said. Then he clucked his tongue.

Opening my eyes, I saw Ken stepping backward. He pulled on the halter, guiding the horse away from the stream. I knew he would be back with another before long. I wondered what Lassiter was doing with Lenora while Ken made sure the horses were watered.

When I was confident Ken was far enough away that he wouldn't hear me, I crawled backward until a tree hid me. I saw the path I left in the snow, so I leaned forward and rubbed it flat. Just as I was finishing up, I heard Ken on his way back.

I pressed my back to the tree, taking long, slow breaths. My hand compress was wet and starting to slip. I didn't bother trying to fix it. Ken was almost back to the spot he'd been at minutes ago. I could hear his voice, low enough that I couldn't tell what he was saying. I figured he must have been talking to another horse.

His voice grew in volume the nearer he got to me. Soon, I could hear him clearly.

"Get you a sip," he said. "Make it quick. I want a sip myself. Of the whiskey."

He let out a barking laugh that caused the horse to neigh.

"Go on and drink, damn you." I heard a light smacking sound, probably Ken's hand against the horse's backside. There was a snort, then silence. A moment later, Ken said, "There. Drink up."

I was trapped where I was. As much as I wanted to sneak around the other side and make my way up to Ken, I knew I couldn't do so without being seen. What I needed to do was wait until he left again. Then I could slink closer to where he was bringing the horses and wait for him. I figured he had one more to bring over. Maybe not, for all I knew. But I assumed there were three horses—one for Lassiter, Ken, and Ahote. Unless they made Ahote walk the entire way to our camp. I doubted that, though. He probably had a horse.

But that didn't mean Ken hadn't already watered the other two. Far as I knew, this horse was the third and he would be staying at the camp for the rest of the night. That would make sneaking up on them even harder. If I could somehow handle Ken alone, I could go after Lassiter afterward. Lenora and me against one leaned a bit more in our favor.

I almost laughed at my thinking process. I was acting like some kind of outlaw—a killer. I had already decided that I was going to kill Ken without really even thinking about it. It bothered me a little that I felt no kind of guilt or even a smidge of indecision. He had to die, and I was fine with that. Just like the others, he was not a person, but a monster of his own doing. Killing him was like putting down a mad dog.

But the one aspect of my decision I hadn't taken

into consideration was that I would have to actually be in a position to do the deed. All would be for naught if I couldn't pull it off.

I heard Ken speak again and realized his voice sounded further away. I risked a peek around the tree. Sure enough, Ken's back was to me as he guided the horse up the side of the stream. I was tempted to have a go at him now, but I figured there was too much distance for me to cover just to reach him. He would probably hear me, turn around, and put a bullet in my chest before I got close enough.

I waited another minute or so before moving. I went around the right side of the tree, pushing bowed branches out of my way to get to the other side. I could see the trampled patch of snow where Ken had brought the other horses to. There was nothing for me to hide in—no brush or dens underneath sagging branches. The space was wide open.

I scanned the area multiple times, trying to locate *any* nook or hollow I could slip into. I even considered burying myself in the snow. Ken seemed dumber than a pile of donkey shit, but I figured even he was smart enough to notice a large mound had suddenly formed in the snow nearby.

I looked up in the trees. I saw plenty of branches reaching outward in all directions. There were some good spots up there, but I would have to climb pretty high up to get to them. Then a kid—me—would have to trust himself enough to drop down from higher up and somehow land on top of Ken without further injuring myself. Plus, the trees would be slick and trying to shimmy up one of them with a wounded hand would be next to impossible.

So, that eliminated that as a possibility.

I stood there, gnawing at my crusty bottom lip. I was out of luck. There was nowhere I could go. I turned around and stared in the direction Ken had gone. I could see the smoke of their fire rising into the darkening sky. It was nearing dark. Soon, the light would start to wane. That would surely help with hiding, but I knew Ken wouldn't be coming out to water any horses in the dark.

Probably wouldn't be coming back out here at all. I supposed I was right in my thinking that he had just finished with the third horse. Or there hadn't been a third horse at all.

Ken wasn't coming back.

Just as I began to curse my defeat, I heard Ken's voice again. Through the swirling snow, I could make out the vague shape of Ken and something much larger beside him, shuffling at a meager pace.

The third horse. That would be the last one, too. This was it.

My only chance to get this right.

24

I DECIDED THAT just standing here and waiting for him might be my only choice. Maybe seeing me would shock him into a momentary stupor that would allow me to use my knife on him.

"No way in hell," I muttered.

Ken would either shoot me or call out to Lassiter. Either way, I would have failed.

He was even closer now. A few more steps and he would probably be able to see me. I needed to go. But where?

I turned around and flung my hat into the trees. Without thinking twice, I stepped down into the stream. The water covered me up to my knees. At first, my pants shielded me from the harsh cold. Then it began to soak through the fabric, feeling as if I were being slashed with icy blades.

Hissing through clenched teeth, I shuffled out a couple steps. I bit down on my tongue to keep myself from hollering. The cold nearly locked me up. I knew if I hesitated for even a second, I wouldn't be able to go any further and Ken would walk up to find me shivering and crying in the stream.

I slid out the knife from behind my back, turned around, and forced myself down on my knees. The water climbed to my chest, hitting me with such a frigid shock that it stole my breath. I could just barely see over the lip of the ground. Ken was almost there. A few more seconds and he would be standing right above me.

I took a deep breath, then sank all the way down until my rump touched the rocks on the bottom. The cold water stung my hurt ear, caused my scalp to tighten as if it were being tugged with a frozen hand. Looking up, I opened my eyes. I could see a crooked stripe of grey surrounded by white smudges. Then two darker shapes appeared in the center of my vision. One was much skinnier than the other.

I didn't think Ken could see me since the water was like liquid shadows flowing through the split in the earth. Had it been a sunny day, the water would have been as clear as glass. Though I figured I might freeze to death, I was thankful I would at least be concealed while I did.

I could see the skinnier shape moving. The larger shape turned, then began to grow until the front of its snout broke through the water. Its tongue lapped less than an inch from my face.

I squeezed the knife in my left hand as tight as I could. I shoved off the rocks with my boots. I crashed through the surface, throwing water everywhere. The horse jumped back with a startled bray. I turned where the skinnier shape had been standing and swung my left arm up and out. The knife hit something hard. There was a slight resistance then it continued to plunge until my fist touched fabric.

Ken was just starting to speak, then his words went out with a gasp as the knife sank into him.

Blinking water out of my eyes, I looked up. Ken was staring down at me, a dumb look on his face. I saw why. He was staring down at the knife I'd pushed into his belly and seemed confused by how it had happened. He looked up at me, his eyes moving from me to the water, then back to the knife. A corner of his mouth lifted.

"Good job, kid," he said. "You made it, eh?"

I nodded. Then I yanked the knife down, splitting his stomach open before pulling the knife out. Ken's mouth dropped open in a look of surprise, his eyes widening. He looked down at his stomach again and began to emit sputtering breaths as his guts sloughed out like bundles of greasy rope. He tried to snatch them before they fell, but the slippery organs slid through his hands. They plopped in the water and floated downstream, slithering past me like lazy snakes.

"Shit . . . " Ken muttered. He dropped forward.

I saw he was coming down too late. I turned to dodge him to no avail. His weight came down on me, pushing me back under the water. My back struck the stones I had been standing on. Their jagged tips scraped me through my wet coat.

Ken turned and spun on top of me but did not move away. I pushed him and only managed to turn him in different directions. I needed to take a breath. I hadn't had the chance to before Ken landed on me. My lungs were burning. Plus, I figured the horse had been startled enough to run back to the camp. I hoped not, but if he had, he would surely beat me there and Lassiter would know something was wrong.

None of that would matter if I couldn't get Ken off

me. I would drown before Lassiter even came to check on things. All he'd find was Ken and me dead and wonder what the hell had happened.

I raised my knees, getting them under Ken's back. He shifted to the left. His arms floated upward. I turned to dodge them only to get smacked in the face by his limp hand. I twisted to the side, moving Ken as I moved. My hip dragged across the stones as I rolled.

Then Ken slid over even more, freeing me. I shoved him away, then launched myself upward. I tore through the water and took a deep breath of cold air. It stabbed my lungs as it went in. I started coughing and feared I might never stop. Eventually, I did. Each time I took a breath afterward, it sounded wheezy and gargled.

Something nudged the side of my head. Without looking, I knew it had to be a gun. Lassiter had been alerted and had already come here. I slowly turned my head, preparing to be looking down a barrel.

And was met by two large nostrils puttering warm air against my face.

The horse hadn't run off, after all. He sniffed me a few times before moving past me to drink from the creek. I patted his neck and realized I no longer had the knife.

"No . . . " I turned and stared through the water, hoping to spot it. I did not want to go under again. I didn't even grab one of Ken's guns before shoving him away.

"Stupid, Billy. So stup . . . "

Ken's body emerged from the bottom of the stream, facedown, his arms stretched out. He was only a few inches from me. I saw a familiar handle secured behind his back through his belt. I rushed over and grabbed him before he could float away. It took a few tries, but I managed to tug out the pistol from his back.

It was Daddy's Colt.

Feeling its cold steel in my even colder hand filled me with a magical warmth. Even when I saw my makeshift bandage was gone and the horrible condition of my hand, I didn't falter even a bit. The flesh of my severed nubs had peeled back to show broken bone. It didn't matter to me. I had Daddy's gun.

And I was going after Lassiter.

25.

I HAD ONLY walked a few feet before the cold became too much. I was soaked, moving through blasts of frigid wind. The water on my skin quickly froze, leaving strips of ice on my sleeves. Each step became harder to perform. My legs felt leaden. I half expected to freeze in place and be stuck there until warmer weather caused it all to thaw.

My clothes felt like sheets of ice pressed against my cold skin. Each movement hurt, but I didn't dare stop walking. I knew if I did, I wouldn't be able to start back up again.

The path was a short distance to the camp. It might as well have been ten miles from how long it took me to cross it.

Reaching the edge of the woods, I stood partway behind a tree and peered into the camp. The other two horses stood off to the side, covered in heavy blankets. The fire crackled, the flames high and flapping. I saw nobody sitting around it.

I made my way in, moving slow and quiet. As I neared the fire, the heat swarmed over me. I gritted my teeth to keep from sighing in delight. Beyond the fire was a makeshift tent much like the one McCray and Floyd had built for themselves. This one was smaller, though, barely able to contain the two people inside.

A pair of pale, bare legs stuck out from the mouth of the tent, parted wide while a pasty, naked ass thrusted between them. With each shove, the buttocks clenched. I heard Lassiter grunting through his laughter. Of course I knew my sister was the one being attacked like that. Though she made no noise at all, I knew she didn't want to be there.

What the fire didn't warm on me, the anger that boiled inside took care of. I began to shake, but not from the cold. I raised Daddy's Colt, leveling it on the tent. As much as I wanted to fire a shot right through the crack of his disgusting ass, I didn't want to risk hurting Lenora.

I thumbed back the hammer. The click resounded over Lassiter's merriment, silencing his laughter. He stopped thrusting.

"Ken?" he said.

"No," I said.

"Billy?" Lenora said through a gasp. "That you?"

"Yep."

"I'll be damned," said Lassiter. He chuckled. "Damn, boy. Yer somethin' else, huh?"

"Billy! Look ou—"

Lenora's warning was cut off by a loud boom that ripped a wide hole through the side of the tent. Through the flapping gap, I glimpsed a bright flash, illuminating my sister and Lassiter. She was on her back, naked with Lassiter crouched over her, his left arm stretched out in my direction.

The wood in the fire exploded from the impact of the bullet, showering my face with hot embers. Had there not been a mask of ice already there, my skin may have ignited. Spinning away, I dropped to my knees and pointed the Colt toward the tent.

Lassiter was no longer on his knees with his bare ass stuck out in the cold like a dog digging up a den of bunnies. The cloth walls of the tent shook as Lassiter growled words I couldn't quite understand.

"Where's Ken, boy?"

"Dead."

"Liar!"

"Wouldn't he have come running by now if he wasn't?"

Lassiter seemed to consider this for a moment. Then he said, "You little shit!"

Another shot rang out. I heard it whisk by above me, missing me by at least two feet. Lenora let out a squeal, then Lassiter cursed. There was a smacking sound that I knew came from Lenora being struck by his hand.

I rolled onto my stomach, wanting to shoot into the tent so much I shook from more than the cold. My clothes were heavy and sagged against me, making me even angrier.

"You killed Ken?" said Lassiter. "How?"

"Gutted him."

"Bullshit."

"Go see for yourself. He's floatin' downstream right about now!"

"You got a lot of guts yerself, kid. We's gonna see 'em soon enough."

"Let Lenora go and come try it."

I couldn't believe the tough words that were spitting out of my mouth. They came naturally, without any provocation or prior thought. I wanted to sound dangerous, but I knew my squeaky voice made it difficult to take me very seriously. No wonder he doubted I'd actually killed Ken. He had to know that I'd done *something* to his partner, or he would have shown himself by now.

"So what we gonna do here, kid?" said Lassiter. "I got yer sister in here, and I reckon you got me dead to rights from out there."

"Yep."

"So what we's gonna do 'bout it?"

"I'm gonna kill you," I said. "Just like Ken."

Lassiter laughed. "Big talk fer a kid whose sister I could snuff out right now."

I felt a sharp tug in my stomach at the threat to Lenora. I knew he *could* do it anytime. He had all the power inside that tent. What I wasn't so sure about was if he actually would. He'd made it clear how badly he'd wanted Lenora. Until I'd showed up, he was having her. I knew he wouldn't want that to end, even if I'd killed a hundred of his men.

"Tell you what," he said. "We's comin' out. I'd hold my fire, if'n I was you."

Lenora shambled out of the tent, looking two heads shorter than normal. She still wasn't dressed, and she'd gained another arm around her throat. She hobbled on her knees forward with Lassiter doing the same behind her. I could just barely see his eyes peeking over the curve of Lenora's shoulder.

I adjusted my aim, but since I wasn't left-handed naturally, my arm trembled as I tried to hold the shot. I knew firing was a bad idea. If my right hand was in better condition, I would have tried for it without thinking.

Shivering, Lenora tried to cover herself, but it was hard for her to do from the way Lassiter held her against him. He put the pistol's barrel under her chin, pushing so she had to tilt back her head. I saw the slant of her neck, denting inward from the pressure of the barrel.

"What we gonna do, kid?" he said again.

"Don't really know," I said.

"You look wet."

"The creek."

"Ah." Lassiter studied me. "Yer likely to catch yer death in this cold and snow."

I didn't have anything to say to that. I figured there was a good chance I already had during the short walk from the creek to the camp and just didn't know it yet.

Lassiter sighed. "You know you ain't walkin' away from this."

"I don't know," I said.

"How'd you get away from yer camp?"

"It wasn't easy."

"Bet not. Did Mommy get her belly full?" Lassiter snorted.

I ignored the anger his comment stirred inside me. "Where's our father?"

"Back at my camp, with the others. They's all waitin' fer me to get back. Probably think I'm dead out in this shit."

I wanted his crew's thoughts to be accurate and would do whatever it took to make sure they would be.

"Is he alive?" Lenora asked. Her voice sounded tired and hoarse.

Lassiter snorted again. “Maybe.”

Lenora looked at me. “Shoot me.”

At the same time, Lassiter and I said, “What?”

“You heard me, Billy.”

“I’m not gonna . . . ”

“Yes, you are. You’re going to do it.”

Lassiter laughed. “Yer shittin’ me, girlie. You don’t want yer brother to shoot you no more than I want him to. But I will you shoot you both, if I feel like I have to. And I’m startin’ to think it might just be easier. After all, all yer holes still work even if yer dead.” He really laughed at that remark.

“I’d rather you do it than him,” said Lenora. She was talking to me, staring me right in my eyes. I could tell she meant it. “If we’re gonna die here, you should be the one to do it.”

“I . . . ” I shook my head. I didn’t like hearing Lenora talk that way. But I understood where it was coming from, though I shouldn’t have been able to at my age. She had given up. All that talk about hope and positive thinking had fled her. She was well aware of the reality and knew that it was bleak.

“Just raise the gun, Billy. Point it at me.”

Lassiter laughed. “Go ‘head, boy. Point that gun. This is a hoot!”

Lenora wasn’t laughing. I wasn’t either, but I was more scared than I had been most of the day, and all day long I had been terrified for my life. I somehow felt cheated. Doing what I’d done just to ensure I got here for Lenora, only for her to ask me to kill her. Didn’t seem fair, on top of all the injustice we’d endured lately.

But if that was what Lenora wanted, then I’d be damned if I wouldn’t give it to her.

I got to my knees, keeping the fire in front of me. If Lassiter tried to take a shot at me he ran the risk of Lenora stopping him. If his arm were to raise, she would be able to get it. I could tell Lassiter was still tempted to try for it, though. His nervous eyes showed me all I needed to know.

I raised the pistol. The hammer was still cocked. I slid my finger in front of the trigger.

Lenora smiled.

"You ain't 'bout to shoot yer sister," said Lassiter. For the first time, I detected a hint of doubt in his voice. He wasn't so sure anymore. "It's ridiculous to even think you might."

"I don't want to do this," I said to Lenora. "I don't."

"I know. But you will?"

I nodded.

"Good. I love you, Billy."

I was opening my mouth to say it back when she winked at me. That struck me as odd right away. It was the same kind of thing she would do whenever she was trying to pull something on somebody and caught me staring at her for clarification. It was her subtle acknowledgment, to let me in on a joke even if I didn't know what the punchline was.

But I knew it was coming. She just needed my attention so I wouldn't miss it.

"I love you too," I said. I straightened my arm, straining with all I had to keep it steady.

"I'll be damned," said Lassiter, thumbing back the hammer on his pistol. "Kid, let's talk about this."

I made a motion that I was about to fire, keeping my finger steady over the trigger. It was the action

Lenora had been waiting for. She went limp in Lassiter's hold, dropping as if all the weight had shifted to her knees. Her naked body sank to the ground, yanking Lassiter forward with it. His arm was pushed aside, opening him up to me.

Lassiter realized what had happened a moment too late. He started to adjust his aim, bringing his pistol back toward Lenora who now lay at his feet. I didn't give him the chance to finish the movement.

I fired.

26.

THE GUN JUMPED in my hand, throwing my arm back at me. The barrel whacked the bridge of my nose. My head was knocked back. I saw the sky turning above me, then my back crashed to the ground. I don't know where the gun went.

I tried to sit up, but my vision was spinning. I could only lay there and listen to Lassiter hollering.

"I knew it!" he shouted. "Fuckin' kid! Damn bitch! I knew—"

There was a solid sound of metal striking something not as hard. Lassiter let out a grunt, followed by a thud of something heavy hitting the ground.

"You okay, Billy?"

I wasn't so sure, but I told her I was. Then I added, "I could have *killed* you!"

"I was starting to think you were actually going to shoot me. Figured I needed to wink at you, so you'd know that wasn't my intention."

"I sure thought it was at first. Is he . . . ?"

"No. You got him in the shoulder. I knocked him out. Can you sit up?"

I didn't think I could but told her I'd try. When I first started to move, my stomach flipped. There was nothing left to come up, though, so I only burped a nasty taste that singed my throat. I got upright from the waist up with my legs extended in front of me. The fire was dying down, and I could see Lenora and Lassiter without any trouble. She stood next to Lassiter, holding his pistol down so the barrel pointed at his bandaged head. Lassiter was on the ground, eyes narrowed and mouth hanging open. The wrap on his face had come loose, sagging over his face. He looked dead, but I figured he was only knocked out.

"Where're your clothes?" I asked.

"In the tent. Get your gun and watch him while I get dressed."

I looked around. Daddy's pistol was on the ground within reach. I grabbed it. "Okay."

"Be right back," she said, then ducked into the tent.

She returned a few minutes later, wearing her clothes and boots. I noticed there were fresh rips and tears that showed patches of her pale skin. Lassiter must have been very eager to get her clothes off.

Lenora saw that, like Lassiter, I hadn't moved. "You all right?"

"I don't feel too good."

"Stay there by there the fire."

Lenora walked over to a sack that was leaning against a tree near their horses. Keeping Lassiter's gun in her hand, she reached in with the other to tug out some branches. She carried them to the fire and added them. It didn't take long for the hungry flames to start eating.

She stood over me. "You're going to have to get out of those wet clothes."

"I can't be . . . naked."

"They have clothes you can put on. I might borrow some myself, for that matter."

"Fine."

Lassiter moaned. We both looked over at him and saw he was starting to sit up. As he did so, the wrap fell loose, sliding down his shoulders and exposing his scarred face. He had no hair anywhere save for some fuzzy patches that seemed to have been hardened into the scabby places. His flesh looked like melted candlewax that had hardened again into a lumpy mold that spread over his entire head. His left eye was hollow darkness, but his right seemed fine, and it looked over at us.

Lenora pointed the pistol at him. "Don't move."

"Don't think I can, darlin'." He put his hand on his bleeding shoulder. "I'm hurt." He looked down at the mound of bandages and sighed. "And you've seen my face." That realization seemed to drain the rest of the fight from him. "Damn."

"Where's our father?" asked Lenora. "Tell us the truth."

Lassiter shrugged, then groaned. "Ouch." He rubbed his shoulder. Blood flowed over his fingers. "We had him and the redskin fight. The winner got to go with us to yer camp. Promised to spare the family of whoever won." Lassiter let out a soft chuckle.

Lenora swallowed. It made a dry clucking sound. "Ahote won."

"Hell no. He lost. Yer paw's a good fighter. Was, a good fighter."

"Was?" Lenora asked. She looked at me. Tears made her eyes shimmer.

I felt an empty space open in my chest that seemed to suck my heart into it.

Was.

"I wanted him to lose," said Lassiter. "So I shot him myself. He could'a killed that Indian, but he chose not to. Good heart, yer paw, but damned stupid. If he'd killed the redskin like he shoulda done, we'd a been forced to bring *him* with us instead." Lassiter laughed again, but his disfigured mouth barely moved. "There's a word fer that. I think it's called . . . "

Lassiter never got to say the word, though years later I figured it out.

Irony.

He never got to reveal it to us that night because Lenora stopped him by putting a bullet through his head. At that close of range, the bullet made a small hole going in but seemed to blow the other half of his head apart as it came out.

Though that single shot had killed him, it didn't stop Lenora from putting two more rounds into his head after he was down. I didn't even bother trying to fire my gun. I no longer had the strength to lift my arm.

The horses also didn't seem bothered by this, for they made no sounds or even flinched when Lassiter was killed.

I stayed on the ground while Lenora gripped Lassiter's ankles. The same way Wally had dragged away Ahote, she moved Lassiter away from the camp. She left him behind some trees. When she returned, she walked over to a sack that had been propped near the fire. Opening it, she dug around inside and removed some clothes. Even from where I was, I could tell they were filthy and much too big for me.

She walked over to me. "Strip."

I shook my head.

"Don't be modest. I've seen your unmentionables before."

"When I was little."

"You have to get out of those wet clothes. It's freezing out here, and you'll catch your death."

As if to prove her point, I sneezed. She made a face that reminded me of Mama. I started to cry, but I don't think Lenora could tell from how wet and frosty my face already was.

I decided not to waste my energy arguing with her. It was hard getting out of my soaked clothes. They were glued to my skin, and I had to peel them off one section at a time. Lenora tossed me a blanket and I wrapped it out around my shoulders. Though it felt better to be rid of the clothes, I couldn't stop shaking. My teeth chattered hard enough that I thought they might shatter like glass.

"Dry off," she said. "Then put these on." She placed the clothes on a log near the fire. Like our camp, Lassiter and Ken had arranged it the same way. "When you're dressed, we'll go in the tent and buckle down for a cold night."

"Together?"

"We have to. You need to be warm. And so do I. We're going to share the blankets. Now, hurry up."

Lenora turned around, granting me a shred of privacy while I dried off and dressed. When I was finished, I let her know. She faced me again. Her nose wrinkled. "Guess they'll have to do, huh?"

I held up my arms. I was surprised that the clothes didn't feel as big on me as they looked. Especially around the shoulders, they almost felt comfortable.

"They have *some* food," said Lenora. "I saw it. Mostly cans and some jerky. We'll wait till the morning. Right now, we need to get out of the snow. I'll keep checking on the fire throughout the night." She added a few more sticks to the fire, raising the flames to an uncontrolled pitch. She shuffled backward to avoid the scorching tips. "It won't last," she added, as if sensing my worry that she might burn us alive.

Lenora helped me up. She saw my hurt hand and moaned.

"I'd forgotten about your hand," she said. "Damn it. Sit down."

I eased onto the log. Lenora grabbed the bandages Lassiter had been wearing around his head and turned to me. I was already shaking my head before she even took a step. "No. You're not putting that on my hand."

Lenora rolled her eyes. "We don't have time for you to feel icky about it. If they were good enough for his head, they're good enough for your hand."

I supposed she was right about that. Besides, it wasn't like we'd been taking very good care of it before now. Any infection that I might get was probably already beginning to work its way through me. Still, I wasn't too thrilled about it.

Lenora used water from a canteen to wash off some of the dried blood. It didn't hurt, which kind of worried me. Then she made me drink from the canteen while she wrapped my gnarled fingers in the dressing. She tied it in a bow like a gift when she was finished, smiling at me.

I tried to smile back. I couldn't do it.

"Oh," she said, "look what I found in the sack."

She held up Daddy's watch. Seeing it made me feel

so much better. I reached out with a trembling hand and took it. Raising it to my ear, I listened to the soft ticking of time passing. "Lenora?"

"Hmm?"

"Do you think what he said about Daddy is true?"

"Lassiter?" I nodded. She sighed. In a lower voice, she said, "Probably."

I thought it was true. I might have told her so if I hadn't started sobbing. I'd held onto a glimmer of hope that Daddy would somehow still be okay through all this. We lost Mama, but surely Daddy wouldn't have been taken away.

Lenora pulled me into her arms and held me until my sobs turned to quiet snivels. Then we made our way to the tent and got as comfortable as possible. There wasn't much room, so we were cramped close to each other. Lenora wrapped us in a blanket and pulled me close to her, holding me the same way Mama would. She kissed me on the forehead, then laid her head down on the old clothes they'd been using for pillows.

"Thank you for saving me," she said.

I nodded. Heat flowed through my cheeks. "You're welcome."

I knew she wanted to talk about Mama, but she wasn't asking about her. Most likely, she already knew what I'd had to do to get here. I was grateful she didn't bring it up right then because I didn't want to go into detail yet. I needed some space between the incident and telling the story.

Though I was exhausted, I doubted my mind would allow me to sleep.

Turned out, I was wrong. I was sleeping within seconds of closing my eyes.

27.

WHEN I WOKE UP, I was shivering, yet soaked in sweat. The tent was filled with the dim light of early morning. Lenora, leaning over me, had her hand on my forehead.

"Fever," she said. "I was worried about that. Your damn body's burning up so much that I woke up sweating."

My throat felt dry and itchy and swollen. It hurt to swallow. "What are we going to do?" My voice sounded like it belonged to a stranger—raspy and weak.

"I'll check to see if they have any medicine. And get you some water. Think you can eat?"

I didn't think so and told her as much.

"I'll get you something anyway. Maybe you can nibble on some canned fruit."

Lenora crawled over to the tent's flap that hung askew and pulled it wide. Harsh light poured in, hurting my eyes with its brightness. Gasping, Lenora turned her head away. At first, she looked confused, then her face brightened up to be as vivid as the light.

"The sun," she said.

"Really?"

Lenora crawled out. "Whoo!" I saw her spinning

a circle through the gap between the fabric. “The sky is blue! And the snow’s melting off the trees! Listen!”

I turned my head, pointing my ear upward. I heard the steady taps of dripping water. I couldn’t help but to smile. The sunlight seemed to be here to stay. The snow began to melt off pretty quick, which made it easier for Lenora to search the woods for things to use to aid me. We could have lit out within a couple days, but I was in no condition to travel.

Turned out, I didn’t get to see much of that sunlight because I ended up being really sick. I mostly stayed in the tent for days. Lenora was able to find some medicine in one of the saddle bags, but all it did was make me sleepy. I suppose that was fine because I slept through a lot of the fever. More than once, I thought that I would not wake up again. Each time I did, though, and with a dry throat and a thirst that never seemed to go away.

Then, the night my fever was at its worst, Chenona paid me a visit.

I didn’t know where Lenora was, but the tent was filled with darkness that felt heavy on top of me. One moment, I was staring out a deep blackness, then suddenly she was there. She was devoid of any clothing, her skin glossy and slick. Her hair hung straight and thick around her shoulders. Her face was painted in that skull-like guise as it had been the night she’d died.

I wondered if maybe I was dreaming, but it didn’t seem like I was asleep. Nothing had that strange fuzzy look that dreams seem to have. And I could hear and smell everything as I had been while I was awake. So, I wasn’t quite convinced I was sleeping.

But how was Chenona here?

She was crouched at my feet, legs parted, her knees jutting through the shadows like sleek knolls. Her arms were straight down between her spread thighs. Her breasts were pushed against the backs of her arms.

She stared at me, her eyes blank and empty, an emotionless skull painted across the face of a beautiful woman.

I wanted to flee from the tent, but I felt as if I had been rooted in the ground. I wished Lenora would come in here and find her. Where was she at? Had Chenona done something to my sister? How could she have? Chenona was dead. I watched her jab an icicle into her throat. Lenora and I found her dead body the next morning.

I wanted to ask Chenona why she was here, but I didn't have a voice.

Her arm shifted as she leaned closer, raising her hand. Her finger pointed at me. "You killed them before they were all punished."

I knew exactly what she meant by that—Mama.

Chenona hissed. "You broke the curse. None were able to suffer in their torment. I am trapped in the Empty Land for what I did to them, but you did not allow it be finished. And now you must carry it. One day, you will feast on your own. The fruit of your loins. You will devour the sweet nectar of your own born."

I mustered up every bit of strength I had in me and lifted my head. I looked right at her and said in a loud whisper, "Go away."

Chenona stared at me, wagging her finger. "You carry it now, William Coburn. And when the day comes that you are a father, your hunger will ravage you. Just like the others, you will . . . eat your own baby. And the hunger will never be satisfied."

"Go away," I said again, with more strength behind it. I got up higher, resting on my elbows. I looked her straight in the face and said, "Go!"

Chenona's head tilted to the side. "You pretend that you are not afraid. Fear has a scent and you reek of it, Coburn. I will never leave you. You will take me with you everywhere you go. And when the day finally comes, I will watch your child be born, then I will watch you feed."

I spit at her. "Go away!" I grabbed my blanket, ready to throw it at her. It was all I had nearby that I could use.

As I was about to let it fly, Lenora threw her arms in front of her face to shield herself. "Don't shoot!"

Holding the blanket, I stared at my sister. Chenona was gone. The heavy darkness that drooped over the tent like a curtain was gone. It was morning outside. I could hear birds chittering and chirping throughout the woods.

Lenora lowered her arms. "Is it loaded?" She smiled.

I looked around, confused. *Had* it been a dream? It seemed so real, too real. I didn't even recall waking up, nor could I exactly tell when I had dozed off. It was all bizarre, and I felt strange. There was a buzzing inside my body that I felt just underneath my skin.

"Wild dreams?" Lenora asked.

"I . . . " I looked around one more time, checking for Chenona. She was nowhere around. "I guess it was." Sure didn't feel that way. Though I couldn't see the Indian woman, I could still feel her. Could smell her. It was as she'd said. She seemed to be with me, though I couldn't explain why I felt that way.

That was the first morning I was able to eat something. Lenora managed to shoot a squirrel and fried it up. We ate it with some canned fruit, and I drank two heaping cups of coffee.

We stayed one more day to give me some more time to rest up and recover. The next morning, we packed up what we wanted to take from Lassiter, plus the stuff they'd stolen from us, and lit out.

We traveled along the main path that cut through the mountains. Every now and then, we came up on a shaded area where a swath of ice blocked our way. We took it easy through those sections, so the horses wouldn't slip. Last thing we needed was a horse to bust a leg, or fall over on us and crush us. The sun always seemed to be out now, rapidly melting away the snow. It pelted down from the tree branches above us like heavy rain.

We traveled for three days before we saw another person. Well, two actually. Later, I learned their names were Barney Winscombe and Peter McGee, a pair of miners that had ventured into the woods to hunt for some supper. Barney was rotund with a big pink face and a beard the color of ash. Peter was taller but looked as if there were cornstalks for limbs underneath the heavy clothing.

When they spotted us coming—a lady and a boy, both haggard and beaten leading another horse on a line—they lowered their hands to the pistols on their hips.

"Please," said Lenora. "We need help."

Barney and Peter shared a troubled look, then moved their hands away from their weapons. Barney spoke first, “What kind of hell d’you get caught up in?”

“The worst kind,” said Lenora.

The men looked as if they believed it.

We spent the night with Barney and Peter at their small camp off the trail. We learned they were also heading to Harvest Hill, but had taken the correct route and had only been traveling a week. We told them a bit about our story and after one look at my hand and ear, the men agreed to help us get to the town to find medical help and the law.

Lenora and I agreed that these were good men and we were lucky to have found them.

Traveling with Barney and Peter was much easier since we were going the route meant for travel and not the hellacious busted path that McCray and Ahote had led us onto. We never came across any place known as Devil’s Pass, which meant, we never found Lassiter’s other men or Daddy.

We reached Harvest Hill a few days later.

28.

"THAT'S ONE HELL of a story," said Sheriff Waggoner. He was seated in a chair beside my bed, his legs stretched out and boots crossed.

"Every bit of it's true," said Lenora. She stood over by the window of my room, arms folded over her chest. Most of her bruises had healed. Other than looking a might skinnier, she was almost back to her normal appearance.

Sheriff Waggoner removed his hat to ruffle his greying hair, then put it back on. He had a mustache that matched, curling around his mouth like a frizzy horseshoe. "I know it is," he said. "My men just brought back the bodies this morning. Have to go back out to get the rest."

He removed a cigar from his shirt pocket, clamped it between his teeth, and used his thumb to strike a match. He raised the fluttering flame to the cigar, puffing until it was ignited. Shaking out the match, he leaned forward to look at me.

He cleared his throat. Through a cloud of brown smoke, he said, "I just wanted to hear the story myself, from start to finish."

I had been in the hospital in Harvest Hill for almost a week. I wasn't wrong about infection setting in on my hand. It had to be removed to save the rest of my body from being poisoned. All that remained was a stump that had been dressed in tape. I caught Sheriff Waggoner's eyes looking at it, so I slipped it under the blanket.

"Did you find Chenona?" I asked.

"Chenona? The Indian woman?"

I nodded.

"They found the Indian man, the other kids, and the . . . parents. Plus the body of Wally Calp, a man that's been wanted for murder, theft, and rape. Last known to be riding with Lassiter."

"Not Chenona?"

He shook his head. "No Indian woman. They brought back a pile of bodies, but not her."

A cold, slithering feeling worked through my insides. She was dead. I saw her kill herself. I kept thinking about the night she visited me. I finally told Lenora about it a few days ago and she told me it was the result of a fever dream. I was apt to agree with her, but I just couldn't let myself.

I looked over at Lenora. She was watching me, shaking her head. I took it as her way of telling me not to tell Sheriff Waggoner about the dream. So, I didn't.

"So, kid," said Waggoner, leaning back in the chair. "You killed three outlaws. Four, if you count Jack McCray. There was money out on him, and he'd been doing some business he shouldn't be, but some of the cattle circle pooled some money together for his capture."

"What's your point?" said Lenora with a little more hostility in her tone than there needed to be.

"Well," he said, letting the smoke drift out of his

mouth. “Five hundred for Lassiter, two-fifty each for Wally Calp and Ken Orderson. That’s a thousand. And since the Cattle Circle have been informed of McCray’s demise, they are willing to pay the reward as well. That’s eight hundred on him. So, it looks you, Billy, have a lot of dough coming your way.”

I choked on the words trying to fly out of me. Lenora let out a squeal and rushed over to the bed. She dropped down, bouncing me. I thought she might squeeze the life out of me and inherit the money for herself from how hard she hugged me.

I heard Sheriff Waggoner laugh. “I reckon that’s a little bit of good news for you. Don’t celebrate just yet. I want to go over something else with the two of you.”

From the tone of his voice, I could tell it was back to serious matters. The happiness we shared for that moment was already forgotten.

He cleared his throat again. “We’re not going to share all the details about what happened to you out there. The last thing this town needs to hear about is Indian curses and Wendigos, cannibals and outlaws . . . ” He shook his head. “We’re not going to talk about any of that. The story is Jack McCray was dirty and set you all up to be killed, so he could squander your savings. Only the two of you survived to tell the tale. McCray was killed in the process. Not too far from the truth, just edited a bit to make it easier to hear.”

I had no problem with Waggoner’s request and told him so. Lenora agreed.

“We don’t want anybody knowing what happened to us,” she added.

“Good,” he said. He smacked his thighs, then stood up. “I’ll let you rest, Billy. I’ll be by again to make sure you get your rewards. Nobody else needs to know about that either. Understand?"

I nodded.

"Good. Feel better. You could just grow up to be a mighty fine lawman yourself." He pulled down on the tip of his hat and winked.

I smiled, though I doubted there would be much need for a one-armed lawman anywhere.

Lenora pulled me to her and squeezed me. "We're going to be all right," she said. "Just fine."

And she was right, overall.

Sheriff Waggoner returned the next day and paid me. Lenora hid the money with our belongings and when I'd healed enough to leave two days later, nobody had any indication what we were taking with us.

Waggoner led a party to Devil's Pass and located the rest of Lassiter's goons and arrested them. They returned with Daddy in a pine box that we buried next to Mama in our family plot. We decided to stay in Harvest Hill, since that was where our parents had wanted us to be. Lenora and I lived in a ranch house by ourselves, raising cattle. It was a good life, one that we were used to and one that we should have never left behind.

Lenora never married. Though she never said as much, I figured the reason why she didn't was out of fear that Chenona's visit to me that night might also include any children she could have. Who would want to start a family if that meant your brother would turn into some kind of monster that wanted to eat your kids? Chenona had never mentioned Lenora and I told her that many times, but I don't guess she wholly trusted it.

I didn't, either, for that matter. I also never married. Never went with a girl. Never got a kiss. Never even held a girl's hand.

Don't let that depress you too much. I got used to it. You'd be surprised what you just accept and live with.

Lenora and I made it through life all right. She passed on a few years ago. It's been quiet and lonely here on the ranch without her always nagging me, but I get by. I know my time's coming soon enough. Already, I find it harder and harder to remember certain things. The doctors tell me it's just a matter of months before I don't remember anything at all. A part of me welcomes that, so I will no longer be haunted by what happened. But I know my luck. And that'd probably be the only memory that remained, constantly replaying on a loop that never ends.

I suppose that's the real reason why I felt the need to write all this down, to get the memories out of me, one final time, so they don't go with me to the other side—wherever that may be, or whenever that happens, which will probably be soon. Because I can't imagine living in a world where I don't know who or where I am. I don't think I can let it go that far. Or if it does, how would I even know?

In the meantime, I'll just do what Lenora always said to do.

Focus on the positive things. At least until I have forgotten all about them as well.

THE END

ACKNOWLEDGEMENTS

A very special thanks to my readers for your encouragement and support through the good times and the bad. You all kept me going when I didn't think I could.

ABOUT THE AUTHOR

Kristopher Rufty lives in North Carolina with his three children and pets. He's written numerous books, including Hell Departed, Anathema, Jagger, The Lurkers, The Skin Show, Pillowface, and many more. When he's not writing, he's spending time with his kids, or obsessing over gardening and growing food.

A new website is in the works, but he still can be found on social media.